The Case of the Bitter Draught

Rhiannon D. Elton

The Case of the Bitter Draught © Rhiannon D. Elton 2020
The Wolflock Cases: Book 4
Second edition

ISBN: 978-0-648763-60-4 (paperback)

info@rhiannoneltonauthor.com

Cover compiled by Rhiannon D. Elton

Cataloguing-in-Publication information for this title is listed with the National Library of Australia.

Published in Australia by Rhiannon D. Elton and Pelaia Adventures

Dedicated to those who have taught me the pain of addictions and their cure which lays in unconditional love and love for oneself.

Get More of the Magic & Mystery...

subscribe.rhiannoneltonauthor.com/more

If you want more clues, more magic and more mystery, let me know by going to the Case of the Bitter Draught subscribe page.

You'll get clues, maps, sketches, behind the scenes stories, lore and much more! You'll also be the first to know when a new story is coming out so you can solve the mystery before your friends.

If you sign up with the magical link below, you'll also get a free downloadable map to follow Wolflock's journey to Mystentine University.

subscribe.rhiannoneltonauthor.com/more

Declaration of Intention

Merry meet,

The purpose of the books the author writes is to give representation to as many peoples, creatures and landscapes as they can. Although written from the perspective of a Caucasian teenage boy, the author hopes to offer a light into the harmony of different cultures and creeds of people. The author's aim is to promote harmony, understanding and compassion in all areas, while also inspiring readers to stand up against injustice and be critical thinkers in life.

While the author does their best to research, interview and highlight the best parts of people, they are only human and can make mistakes. The author asks you gently educate them by sending them an email in order to discuss anything that may have caused harm to a group of people unintentionally.

The author believes that the cure for ignorance is education, but please approach the topic cordially in order to avoid any knee-jerk cognitive dissonance.

Finally, the viewpoints displayed in the books comes from a particular character and is not necessarily that of the author's. The author seeks to display flaws, growth and human nature on many levels, and hopes that you will analyse the character of the protagonist without adopting any negative behaviours from them.

Merry part, and merry meet again.

Rhiannon Op Elton

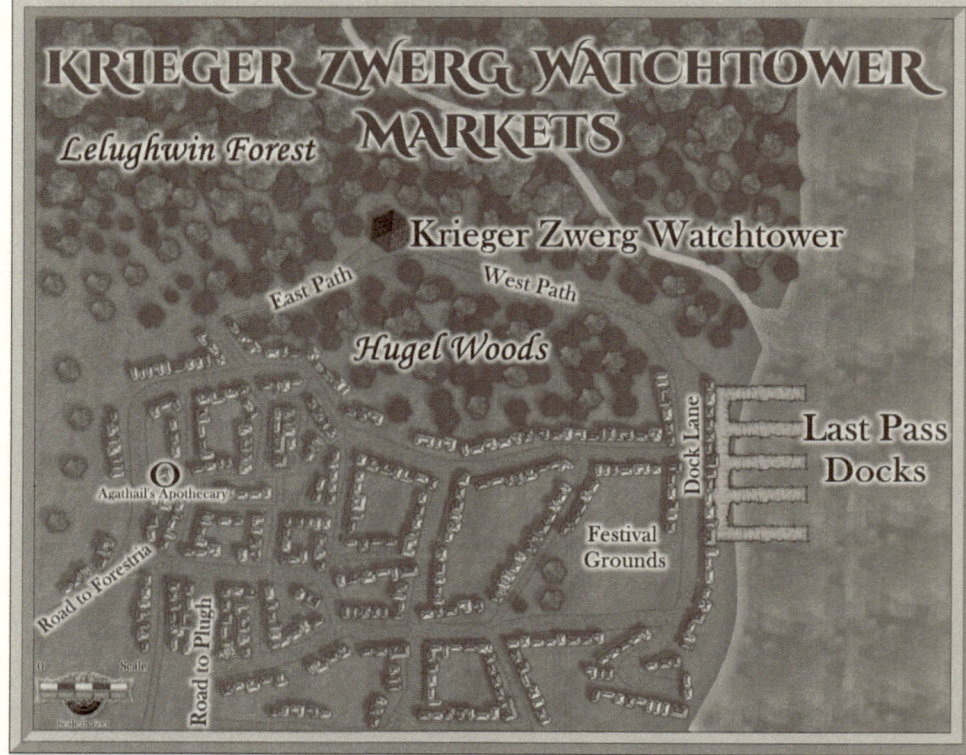

(Excerpt Leevia Asurae's essay on The Ruins of the North and Their True Origins)

The Krieger Zwerg Watchtower is a tower built in the 40th year of the reign of the Evil King Stathan by the newly rescued inhabitants of the North Grothien silver mine. It is said that it was built by Svartalfar (Mountain Dwarves), but there is no primary evidence suggesting this is accurate.

It became an essential lookout post for war ships heading to Shiriling, giving the rebellion the ability to ambush King Stathan's forces. It is said he lost twelve legions of soldiers before he could be convinced to cease his attacks by river and sea.

Although now a post office, scholars still regularly make sketches of the thousands of sigils carved into each stone in order to further magical research. The reason for this is due to the suspicion that the Krieger Zwerg had some of the best distraction, illusion and defensive magic still known to this day. All claims have been currently unverified, but studies are hopeful...

CHAPTER 1
Mischief at the Markets

Wolflock hated Mabon.

As far as he was concerned, it was a silly festival. It only existed to remind farmers to do whatever it was they needed to do and make everyone who wasn't a farmer feel bad. The day was as long as the night, but it only made the night feel longer than it should.

Everyone played balancing games, ate freshly harvested Autumn foods and talk about how thankful they were. The focus was meant to be on what they have sown and reaped for the year. Wolflock had terrible memories of his aunties telling him that everything he was thankful for wasn't something he should be thankful for. They always said he should be grateful for his family, friends or other nonsense. Wolflock's only friends for years had been his sister, Myna, and his horse, Brennan, which he didn't feel the need to thank. None of the house staff were interesting enough to hold his attention, and his father was always shut away in his office working. So, he didn't believe they deserved any extra gratitude.

He remembered his old nanny would pick out the most atrocious frilly outfits. The kind of garb he couldn't get up to any mischief in if he didn't want to tear the delicate dangly lace. His father was the wealthiest of his siblings, which meant he was socially obligated to have the entire Felen family come stay with them for a fortnight or longer, which to Wolflock was a fortnight too long. It was a requirement to lay out far too much food at the Mabon dinner to show how abundant the year had been. Before they ate, everyone would be forced to join hands and tell the room what they were thankful for as if it were some kind of competition in humility.

Only his father took the event seriously. He often said practical things like, "Our dedicated staff..." or "the health of our horses...". He also always said, "My wife and children...", which was probably why he always went first. The impending sense of gloom created by the empty seat to his left would be dispersed by the time Wolflock ruined the evening. His aunts would say stupid things like "My amazingly clever daughter", even though his cousins had no intellectual aptitudes. Nor did they have any desire for extended education either. Sometimes they'd fawn over their new husbands and mewl something stomach churning like, "The love of my life", when next season they'd change partners like they did fashions.

Then it would come to Myna, who knew exactly what to say, even from the age of three. She would be grateful for whatever immediate gift their aunts had brought her, as well as recite the uses of the last Mabon's gifts and how she'd used them. Wolflock would roll his eyes as far as they would go and make gagging faces to no one's amusement.

Then it would be his turn.

Firstly, he would be stumped. Nothing he said would be good enough. His horse would be scoffed at because he said it every year. His musical instruments would be sneered at because no one had gifted them to him recently, and he refused to play them for his family's amusement. His books incurred eye rolls because "good boys didn't spend all day reading". It would always happen the same way. Wolflock would say he was grateful for something he actually was grateful for. One of his aunts would roll their eyes and snap, "You can't be grateful for that!" and Wolflock would retort with why he was more grateful for "that" than anything anyone else around the table had said.

And it would be on.

Everyone would start yelling except for Myna, who would be trying to soothe the situation while also getting smug glee at the drama. Their father would ask the youngest children if they would pass the gravy while calmly eating his meal.

So, when the Captain announced that their last stop for the better part of a month would allow them to pick up supplies for that evening's Mabon celebrations, Wolflock felt like someone had poured egg yolks down his back. Memories of hiding away in the stables for as long as possible, complaining to Brennan that he was grateful for nothing and wished his mother was here to tell them he was allowed to say whatever he wanted to say, came flooding back to him. His body grew tense and his mind sparked with every way this could go wrong.

He sat at dinner that evening, feeling sullen and without an appetite. Mothy hadn't attended dinner with everyone else as he was still recovering. Wolflock thoroughly believed that his friend's slow recovery had more to do with him still being tended to by Nü than with him still being ill. He picked up a bowl of vegetable stew for Mothy and left the buzzing excitement of the dining hall. He was too agitated about the next evening's events to try to maintain pleasantries.

As he descended the stairs to the cabins, he heard Nü's tinkling laugh.

"... And that's when I realised curry has more power than anyone should ever be allowed to wield."

Nü snorted and guffawed like a donkey, making Wolflock chuckle. He opened the door without knocking and Nü jumped up in surprise, tearing her hand from Mothy's. Both their faces turned three shades pinker.

Wolflock smirked.

"Brought you dinner, Sir Sickness. I figured you wouldn't want any, Nü, since you normally make your own."

Mothy coughed and his face lightened. "Brilliant! I'm starving. Is this ok to eat, Nü-mei?"

Nü went to speak but stopped, her lips parted, and her sharp dark eyes blinked wide in surprise. She blushed even more and, after a moment, giggled behind her hand.

"Did I use that right?" Mothy grinned as Wolflock pressed the stew into his hands. "Nü's been teaching me how to speak central Xiayahn."

"Is that so?" Wolflock raised an eyebrow. "I bet it

takes a long time to get your tongue around those tricky pronunciations."

"You did use it right," Nü interrupted, shooting Wolflock a warning glare. "But do not let my father hear you call me that. He will... well... he will think we are engaged."

Mothy choked on his stew and Wolflock burst out laughing.

"It means 'pretty' though, right? We call people pretty and sweet down South all the time!" Mothy protested.

Nü giggled her chime-like laugh again, "That is fine, but in Xiayah we only use that term with people we are very close to and have known for many years. I will go and make my own dinner now."

"Can I still call you Nü-mei when your father isn't around?" Mothy leaned forward, his eyes glittering with hope.

Nü stood by the door, her plain green and brown dress contrasting with her porcelain skin and her obsidian hair. She rested a dainty hand on the doorframe and barely looked back over her shoulder. She bit her lip, smiled, and nodded before she slipped out, closing the door behind her.

Wolflock looked from the door to Mothy and

started to feel his previous frustration grow again. Was Mothy really going to pass him off during this wretched festival too?

"I guess I'm just superfluous now."

"I do not know what that means but you can be anything you want to be," Mothy sighed and rested back on the bedhead wall.

Wolflock shook his head, leaning back on the wall adjacent. There was a long moment of quiet before Mothy started eating his food.

"Captain says we're having Mabon celebrations after we stop at the last port tomorrow."

"Sounds good. Should be fun. You gonna buy anything?"

Wolflock shrugged.

"I might do an hour's work or so and pick up some presents for everyone. You should join me."

Wolflock shrugged again. He'd never had to buy presents for anyone except for Myna, and even then, they were only the books he knew she'd like.

"The food should be good. They might pick up a roast."

Wolflock pulled a face. He could already smell the sickly sweet pork roast with undercooked crackling his aunts would insist on making. Wolflock liked pigs. They were cleverer than goats or sheep, so he didn't enjoy eating them. Also, the fresh meats tasted bland, so they often had to be salted far more than other meats. He wasn't particularly enthused about anything too sweet or too salty.

"What are you looking forward to?"

Irritated by the question, Wolflock heaved himself up and took up Mothy's empty bowl.

"For it all to be done and dusted."

Mothy followed him out with no shoes on. "Let's play cards. I'm bored and I want the company."

Wolflock rolled his eyes as they emerged back onto the deck under the starry night sky. "You know you can't beat me? You have so many tells. I can guess what's in your hand right away."

"Not if we play snap."

The evening passed faster and with sore, slapped hands. But the impending Mabon still darkened Wolflock's mood. Especially when the crew started organising the menu at the table Mothy and Wolflock were playing at. They brought out paper leaves, a tight rope game, hoops and balls, baubles and all different shades of orange, brown, yellow, and red streamers. As they hauled up the boxes, the colours spilled out across the dining hall floor.

Finally, Wolflock had had enough and went to bed

in a restless mood, thinking maybe he'd wake up and it would all be over.

The next morning proved him wrong.

He was normally one of the first passengers to wake up, but there was hustle and bustle all around. He heard footsteps and chatter above. Barrels being rolled back and forth. Creaking wood and ropes, as well as the other passengers chatting in the hallway. A new noise seemed to come through Wolflock's window. Seagulls... and... livestock?

He groaned as he rolled out of bed, wiping the sleep out of his eyes. Outside his window was...

Barrels.

Stacks of barrels. *How utterly boring.*

Wolflock resigned himself with a sigh. Since they'd be going ashore and meeting new faces, making transactions and socialising, he thought it best to at least dress well. As he pulled on his long-sleeved white shirt, he felt a flash of gratitude for the trick Mothy taught him about hanging his clothes while they were still wet to drop out the wrinkles. He'd hate to be seen out of Plugh looking less than decent. He buttoned his swirling silver and black vest, pulled on his slacks, and wiped his shoes. He opened the window to test the weather and felt a bitter chill. It was a nippy Autumn, indeed. Digging through his trunk he drew out his jacket. The collar was too short, and it didn't reach his thighs, but it would have to do.

"I guess I'll have to purchase warmer clothes..."

Wolflock gave his black hair a quick comb and set out. The company looked much like they did the first day Wolflock had boarded the Silver Ice Hair. They moved about, conversing from their doorways and visiting one another's rooms. But this time, instead of looking frustrated, they all looked excited.

Mothy's door was open and the blonde boy was trying to peek around the barrels obscuring his window as he buttoned his chestnut vest.

"Good morning," Wolflock huffed.

"Mornin'," his friend grinned broadly back at him. "Captain'll let us off soon. They just have to do their side of things first."

"Their side of things?"

"Yeah. You know. Log everything going off and organise what's coming on that's ship cargo. Get new stuff for anything that's broke. Oh! And get more food!"

Wolflock nodded, crossing his arms as he leaned on the doorframe.

"How long are we stopping for?"

"Just til after lunchtime, I think. We'll have time."

Something about Mothy's tone was apologetic. It

wasn't about wanting to go shopping around the markets. It was something else...

"You offered to help someone before you left the ship, didn't you?"

Mothy shrugged sheepishly. Something about the way Mothy said nothing made Wolflock think there was more.

"You offered for both of us to help?"

It had to be someone on the ship, likely a crew member. The ship's primary focus had been on the Mabon festivities. Wolflock could deduce that it would only be to do with the kitchens or the decorations. A lot of the food and some decorations still had to be collected ashore, so it was likely cleaning. Which meant their indentured chores could only be on the ship, limiting the precious time they had on land.

"We're helping Grogen clean the kitchen, aren't we?"

"Glad to see you didn't balk at the-" Wolflock stared at him with his arms folded and his eyes stony. "... Well, if we get started now then we may be able to leave soon... We can go up now if you like?"

With an exaggerated sigh, Wolflock rolled his eyes and let Mothy grab his brown baker boy hat before he led the way. Wolflock had grown used to Mothy wrangling him into doing chores around the ship to help the crew. It was significantly more entertaining than remaining bored and idle. Wolflock often stopped halfway through their work and just listened. He found observing gave him more details than if he had worked as diligently as Mothy. As much as he wanted to see the new port, it relieved him to not have to think about the subsequent shopping for Mabon for a while. He could just pretend everyone would forget about it. He could pretend it was just a normal day onboard.

When they arrived in the kitchen, Wolflock was thankful that Grogen was just as eager to get off the ship as everyone else was. The burly man had been working since the early hours to make the kitchen spick and span. He'd been preparing all the dishes needed and taking stock of all the food and menu items for the festival and final leg of their journey.

"Ah! Lads! Glad yeh could make it. Now, ta finish up, we just gotta take out the last lot o' bread, hang up the clean pots and check what we're missing for tonight. I know what we need, so I'll go to the hull. Can I trust you two ta not burn the bread?"

"So, charcoal is cooked right?" Mothy smirked, looking into the oven and smelling the freshly baking bread.

Grogen tapped him up the back of the head, flicking his straw-coloured hair straight up, chortling. "Black means you'll 'ave to make it fresh at sparra' fart tomorrow."

"How do you set a clock to 'sparrow fart'? Wolflock snickered, looking at his silver pocket watch.

Grogen shook his head and roughed their shoulders affectionately before heading to the hull. Wolflock grabbed armfuls of the pots and pans while Mothy juggled them. One by one, they hung them on the hooks along the walls. When they finished, they both took up some oven mitts with a floral print and waited for the bread to finish baking. Growing bored, they proceeded to have a slap fight. The noise of the passengers rose from outside the dining hall as they began to depart. Wolflock's gut twisted. He wanted to be with them. He needed the distraction. The decorations around the kitchen and dining room had not removed his uncomfortable premonitions of how terribly the night would go.

"Don't check them yet," Mothy warned as Wolflock moved to the oven. "You'll let the heat out and it'll take longer. You have to go by smell." He knelt down to the oven and took a long whiff. "Nope. Not ready yet."

Wolflock hit him with the mitt again, sparking another oven mitt slap fight.

Grogen returned not long after and tapped both of

them on the back of their heads. Wolflock could see he was holding a long piece of paper with the list of things he needed ashore. He also spied a bag filled with coins and metal pieces tied to his hip.

"Have you been saving, Grogen?"

The huge man blinked and glanced down. "Oh! This? Yeh. Bin storing a bit up so everyone can get a gift for Mabon. On the way back, I should have enough to get Yule presents from Creast, too." He patted the chinking bag. "How d'ya figure that out?"

"I'll tell you that if you tell me where you were hiding it. None of the hull's storage allows for crew possessions and there haven't been any coins in the small cupboard beside your bed."

Grogen's face went flat. "Yeh gotta stop goin' through other people's stuff, Mr Felen. S'not polite. And people might pin yeh for a thief."

Wolflock raised his oven mitts in defence. "I swear I steal nothing but knowledge."

Grogen rolled his eyes. "All the crew 'ave hidey holes throughout the ship. When yeh on a moving house with a bunch o' others for such a long time, yeh wanna make a space that's 'specially yours. I got me savin's from me hidey spot. Yeh ain't to know where it is-"

"The compartment under the seventh stair in the

hull? I thought it was thicker than the rest and the wood is newer-"

"Off with yeh both now," he grunted, tearing off their oven mitts and steering them to the door. "And don't be touchin' my things."

"Aye, aye, Grogen," Mothy saluted.

The boys took off at a run to the gangway leading down to the dock. They both stopped when they reached the railing, holding their breath as they took in their clear view of the market.

The Krieger Zwerg watchtower sat high up on a small hill, surrounded by forest with two roads leading down through the thick woods. One road wove South West down to the docks where the ship was nestled. The other headed South East into the strangest town Wolflock had ever seen. Tangled rows of newly built houses and brightly coloured canvas awnings clustered between hard dry dirt roads. Some had stone foundations that looked as ancient as the grey stone tower on the hill. Although their base was old, the wood of the upper portion looked new, as if it had been cut and shaped just a month ago. None of the houses had the glitter of glass in their windows, but each had ramshackle shutters. Several of the larger intersections had hot firepits, sending up plumes of smoke, but none of the houses had chimneys.

As he descended the gangway, Wolflock was hit with the smells of exotic spices, livestock, incense and a medley of various teas. He saw that all the new cargo coming onto the ship were stacked on the dock and was being craned onto the top deck. The mechanism of the large wooden crane fascinated him. A waterwheel turned forwards and backwards under the operator's instruction. Wolflock saw one man pulling and pushing levers, getting everything into position, while another man waved his hand, sending out blue sparks from his fingertips. The sparks shot towards the water, causing it to drive the wheel. Wolflock, who had seen magic plenty of times before, but never showed an aptitude for it, began contemplating how a machine like that could be used without magic.

The mechanism that ascended or descended the crane would have to be separate from the wheel, only reliant on the general motion rather than the direction...

"I've got to go and get some post from the tower," Wolflock broke from his thoughts when he overheard Slavidus talking to Geagle. "Make sure everything is signed for and written down in order."

"Aye, aye, first mate Oncor," Geagle nodded, but his droopy, watery eyes were drifting everywhere except for Slavidus' face.

Wolflock followed his gaze and saw Parihaan, one

of the women from Uluken, scanning over the containers as she made her way into town. He could tell instantly that she was from Uluken by her dress and facial features. She had a delicately hooked nose, light brown eyes, olive skin, and he'd noted thick long black hair when she was adjusting her tan chaarghad headdress. She also wore typical Uluken garments. A long-sleeved fitting turtleneck shirt, a moss green jacket that flared out over her floor-length skirt and leather sandals. Uluken was hot, dry and said to have rolling hills of sand, so the inhabitants dressed from head to toe to stop the sand and save their skin from the blazing sun. As they moved into other climates, it was common that they maintained their dress for quite some time as the air was not as hot and it took them some time to adjust.

"Ah, Mr Felen," Slavidus pointed to him. "You have mail at the tower too. Make sure you collect it before we leave. They'll ring the ship's bell for a good quarter hour, so stay within town and you'll both hear it fine."

Wolflock thought it was odd that he especially had received mail. Had Myna sent him something? Had his father written to him? Was it another attempt at a fine for disturbing the peace before he left? He put it out of his mind as Mothy tugged his sleeve. They nodded to Slavidus as he stepped off, and Wolflock saw Haatji saunter over to the undefended Geagle, batting her long lashes at him. She spoke with her hands, glittering with gold hathphool bracelets. Wolflock couldn't hear what they were saying, but she seemed intent on distracting him from his work.

"Where do you want to go first?" Mothy nudged his arm, and they began strolling down the main road.

"Well, I've never been this far North before, so I'm not sure."

"Captain said the other night that there was lots to see and even more to waste money on."

"You said something about working while we were here to earn some money last night. Any thoughts on that?"

"Oh! Thanks for reminding me." Mothy dug his hand into his trouser pocket and pulled out a handful of wooden coins. They each had a flat pearl disc at their centre and a ring of pearl dust and resin around the edge. "Grogen gave us money as an advance for the work we did for him this morning. Five deimas each!"

"Uh... that's ok. You keep them. I'm not even sure I'll buy anything." Wolflock pulled a face, embarrassed that he had at least a hundred deimas in his luggage on the ship and fifty more in his satchel with him now.

"No, no. You earned it," Mothy shoved the light coins into Wolflock's hand and walked on faster so he

18

couldn't return them. "Captain said that most of the stuff should only cost sentus now, anyway. They are going to hold a festival tomorrow night and start packing up for the Winter and get their fresh stock early Spring. I should be able to get everyone a gift for Mabon."

"Sure... let's just focus on sight-seeing."

They saw half-filled barrels of grain, dried meats hung up on hooks, trinkets and jewellery, clothes and household finery. Some of the more permanent looking stalls were selling hand-carved furniture. Smoke wafted around them in streams from incense cones and sticks, outdoor ovens and fire pits. The smell of tanned leather and all manner of food on sticks slithered like a fat snake throughout the streets. Busking musicians, poets and bards played jaunty and enthralling tales from their woven straw mat stages. Some chased the children up and down the dirt paths to their delighted squeals. Drums beat with a new rhythm on every corner, and instruments from all over the continent played their enchanting tunes for all to marvel at. Each had a beautiful jewelled pot in front of them for people to throw coins into. It was said that the more jewels a performer received, the better they were at their art. People sometimes gave their coins to an ornate pot. Others gave them to an artist with no jewels to help encourage them. Most people just gave a coin to the ones they liked the songs or stories of the most. Wolflock paid for two toffee apples, a custard bun for Mothy, a cup of marinated beef strips, and a bunch of brine boiled carrots to share. Every single store and stall they passed, Mothy ran his hands lightly over the wares in awe.

"It looks so good," he uttered more than once. "Did you make these? You should be so proud! Wolflock, look at this!"

Wolflock stood back and stayed silent. It was all junk. Needless knick knacks that would end up lost or broken in a week. He also ran his hands over a few things, but scrutinised the poor imitation fabrics or glass made gemstones. Nothing really worth anything. Even the books being sold as exclusive printings were all secondhand and not worth the deimas they had on their price tags.

"It's all so pretty! I can't choose."

"Let's head up to the tower and get my mail before it gets too late. And maybe letting breakfast settle will help you think clearly."

They trudged up the hill through the woods to the four-storied stone tower. The woods themselves muted the medley of symbols, guitars and drums thrumming from the little market village. They also seemed to drink up the smells and replace them with earthy damp woody aromas. They made it to the top of the hill, the sounds of music reemerging as the canopy dropped beneath them. The Krieger Zwerg watchtower was a squat thing and didn't look as big as it was from a distance. It was wide at the base and tapered under a newer shingled cone roof, most likely to keep the snow from collapsing it. Wolflock made a private wager to himself that it was at least ninety feet around. As they approached the black metal door entrance Wolflock heard fast steps, a single rolling wheel and muffled shouting from within.

"Watch out for the postboy."

"What?"

He pulled Mothy out of the way, just as a young man around their age ran out, nearly crashed into them. His arms and legs were gangly, and the thick dark gold hair obscured his eyes pushed down over his face by his dusty black flat cap.

"Sorry!" he gasped and kept running.

"And watch out for Nan Ji."

Mothy had stepped in front of the door again, but Wolflock grabbed his shoulder to stop him from being barrelled into. Nan Ji stomped out, looking red faced and fuming.

"Their prices are ridiculous! Do not do business with these creatures!" he snapped, pushing out a large wheelbarrow filled with his herb boxes. Realisation of who he was speaking to dawned on him and he lifted his wide nose and pushed on.

"How did you-?" Mothy gasped.

"I heard him coming."

"But how did you-?"

"He was the most likely to be leaving the tower in such haste."

"But how-?"

"I knew he was a 'he' by the clumsiness and heaviness of his step."

"But then-"

"That shout and silk shoe step are unmistakably Nan Ji's."

Mothy stopped, looking both impressed and miffed at the same time.

"Ahem. Shall we?" Wolflock gestured to the door.

Mothy rolled his eyes. "I don't know. Shall we?"

Wolflock chuckled as he pushed passed. "One day you'll have great deductive abilities of your own. For now, let me have my fun."

The inside of the tower was lined with all manner of pigeonholes. Some even had pigeons in them. Some of the cubbies were bursting with envelopes of all shapes and sizes. Others had brown paper parcels tied with twine stacked on top of one another. Everything seemed eerily still except for a scratching noise from the floor above them.

"Merry meet?" Wolflock announced, not wanting to shock anyone. As he stepped forward, he nudged a pile of envelopes out of the way. "Is anyone there? I was told I have post and I have a few letters to send."

They heard a dull thump, someone cursing and then a pitter patter of feet leading to the stairs. Envelopes on each stair started spilling off the edges, but no one appeared.

"Yes, yes, yes. Merry meet. Merry meet. The post is here to serve," came a gruff voice from the direction the letters had been scattered.

Wolflock and Mothy both looked at one another. Mothy with confusion, Wolflock with suspicion.

"What did you say your name was?"

Silence.

Then a small growl. "Ask us thrice and we'll be nice."

Wolflock smirked. "Is that so? You don't sound like you're going to be nice."

The person sighed. "Really? You're going to do this? Ask us thrice and we'll be nice. Now ask again or this will never end."

"If you ask them their name, you have to ask three

times and then they have to tell the truth, but I hear it irritates them to have anything left incomplete. It's like they get caught in a loop."

"Who on Autumn's name are you talking to? Who are you talking about?" Mothy whispered with wide eyes.

"We have more to do than talk to you. Now ask us thrice to be named and let's be done with this foul game!"

"Alright, alright. What is your name, what is your name?"

They stood still for a moment, waiting, but nothing happened.

"And?" came the disembodied voice.

"And what? I already asked once before."

"Oh! Oh yes. Yes, that's right. Phew. Hogmanx."

"You're invisible, Hogmanx."

With a snapping sound a short squat brown being appeared. It was human in the same way a goblin was. Five fingers and toes, longer than was natural, a short fat round nose and big black eyes. The being was covered in thick follicles of sparse brown hair. It was wearing a tunic, cloth belt and tights that made its small legs look disproportionate to its body. It also only came up to Wolflock's thigh.

"You said you had post?" Hogmanx crossed its arms, tapping its naked hairy foot on the stone step.

"Name and I'll get it."

"Felen. Wolflock Felen."

With a grunt Hogmanx waddled back upstairs and Wolflock turned to an aghast looking Mothy.

"Never seen a brownie before?"

"What is it?"

"Hogmanx is a fairy. Brownies are like the nice version of goblins-"

"We are nothing like goblins! Yuck!" Hogmanx scolded from the room above.

"They like to clean and organise things. If you leave them honey and milk every night, they'll stay. If you forget or insult them, then they leave. I wonder who feeds them here..."

"I've never seen a fairy like that before. I thought they were like the ones we saw on the ship. You know... small and glowy and pretty."

Wolflock shook his head, glancing around at the letters and parcels, trying to make sense of the ordering system.

Who would put Gleichester next to Thranx? Letters to Grothener next to letters to Pyringel?

"Not at all. There are good and bad fairies and they come in all shapes, sizes and disguises. Every nation has its own types. Some are more in this world and you can touch them, others are more like spirits in the next world. I read all about them and a lot of our festivals in Plugh would invite them along so we stayed in their good graces. Otherwise they get up to all sorts of mischief. Turning milk sour, shaving sheep unevenly, breaking eggs, tripping you in the kitchen, stealing babies. That kind of-"

"Stealing babies!?"

Wolflock stopped looking through the disorganised post and stretched. "Well, it's not common. That's why you put iron horseshoes and nails around the baby's crib."

"Don't be talking about that stuff. Yuck!" Hogmanx waddled halfway back down the stairs, "We hate iron. Yuck!" Lifting its long-pointed nose, it sniffed the air. "Felen... Felen... Ah yes."

Hogmanx flicked its long finger out and whipped it back. Like an invisible string was attached to the envelope, it came flying across the room. As it soared through the air Wolflock heard another person come in.

Froderyk scratched his chin as he looked around at the filing disaster.

"Merry afternoon, lads. Collecting your mail?"

"On the contrary. We're teasing fairies," Wolflock snorted.

"Ah. Oh. Hmm... odd choice of fun. Don't spoil the post though. Looks like you've already caused mayhem."

"Oh, this isn't us." Mothy interjected.

"Name?" Hogmanx grunted.

"Timmerman. Mr Froderyk J. Timmerman. I'm only expecting a few letters. Nothing much."

"Timmerman... Timmerman..." Hogmanx sniffed the air in short sharp bursts.

He pointed in the same direction as his nose, then threw out his hand and called over a large box. It was bound tightly so it didn't burst from all the letters inside it.

"Here. Now, shoo."

The brownie dropped the box into Froderyk's arms, whose brow furrowed in concern.

"I... ah... better get on to reading these. See you boys back on the ship..."

"Merry part, Froderyk," Mothy waved as he departed.

Wolflock watched his own letter float around the room in circles as he recalled the origin of the name Timmerman. It meant 'carpenter' in Quarenth.

"Mr Wolflock Felen. Your sister has nice writing. Also, good ink. Not iron. Very good. Now go. Much sorting to do for Hogmanx. Shoo, shoo."

"I'd like to post this one back to her," Wolflock waved his pages.

With a flick of his finger, Hogmanx yoinked them

out of his hand along with a sentus coin.

"You've had your fun, and all is done. Shoo, shoo."

Hogmanx waved them away and the wind seemed to grip them under their arms, dragging them out, Wolflock's letter soaring through the air after them. None of the other papers in the building were disturbed at all. As they landed just outside the entrance, the letter flew right in front of Wolflock's face and hovered there until he took it.

"That was exciting. I wonder if there are any more fairies in the market!" Mothy laughed.

"I certainly hope not. Fairies are tricky. They can't lie and so they tell the truth just enough to get away with their mischief. Best not to talk to them unless you know what kind you're talking to."

The boys made their way back down the path to the market when they heard someone muttering a way off the track. Glancing around, Wolflock spied Slavidus walking in circles around a boulder just inside the woods.

"Psst. Mothy. Look." Wolflock nodded and gestured for them to drop down and creep closer.

They knelt behind a bush and watched.

Slavidus muttered to himself and they could only make out the odd word. Just before Wolflock was going to give up and ask him what was wrong, he finally threw his hands up.

"I can't believe I'm doing this. Why am I doing this? Everything was going so well. Blutro will... I may as well resign. He won't allow it! A dalliance yes, but this magnitude? I... I can't... but... Why did I let him talk me into this... No. That's it. That's it. I'm going to do it. Blutro, be damned."

Wolflock's legs started to ache from the unnatural position he was squatted in. He wanted to slink away, but he didn't think they could without being caught. He tried to reshuffle, but a branch made a resounding crack as he put his knee down.

Slavidus shot up straight and looked around with wide eyes. He sighed as the forest fell back into silence and walked inches from them. They waited for him to be out of sight before rising.

"What was that about?" Mothy asked.

"I'm not sure... yet. Let's head back into town. I would much prefer to watch the performers than sit here any longer. I can't feel my foot."

They made their way back to the market and found themselves in a throng of dancers performing. Their layers skirts, jangling bracelets and tambourines made for an exciting display. Two of the girls dragged Wolflock and Mothy into the dance and span them in circles. Wolflock retreated to the sidelines, but Mothy joined wholeheartedly. He clapped and skipped along, pulling Wolflock back into the fray. Midway through the dance Mothy stopped and grabbed Wolflock's arm, pulling him through a small alley.

"Lockie! That's it! That's what I want to get everyone."

Wolflock looked at the store he was pointing at. It was one of the more permanent stores with a stone foundation and a rough wooden awning. Strings of dried herbs lined the awning and open windows. Bags of seeds slouched against the wall and the smell of potions being brewed seeped out and around them. Unlike most of the other stalls, there was not a single living person browsing the wears. Hanging from a pair of iron chains was a rough-cut sign with the words "Agathail's Apothecary", carved and chipped into the old dead wood.

"Perfect! I know just what to get them all."

Wolflock made a face, not hiding how dubious he was about this location. They entered through a door of dangling wooden beads and heard the bubbling of the potion being made. Shelves lined the walls, each with potion vials, jars of dried specimens, pot plants, taxidermied animals and other bric-à-brac. Over the bubbling cauldron leant a tall woman with the frizziest hair

Wolflock had seen. It was tied back in a ponytail that floated like a brown cloud behind her sun beaten face. Possibly in her forties, her long-nailed hands stirred the brew, her sleeves rolled back to her elbows, revealing intricate overlapping lines tattooed from her hands up.

"Merry meet, boys. What are you seeking?" the woman said in a smooth voice.

"Merry meet, ma'am. I'm looking for a particular seed. I'd like a bag of about ten seeds for thirty people and maybe a few extras of another kind."

"And what seeds be they?"

Mothy glanced at Wolflock and made a shooing motion with his hands. "Let me speak with her in private so the surprise isn't spoilt."

"Alright. But just so you know, I'm not getting you anything so don't bother about me."

Mothy just rolled his eyes and continued shooing until Wolflock retreated to the back of the store where the counter was. Behind the dusty counter was a small money chest and a tattered ledger. Wolflock glanced over, seeing the backs of Mothy and the woman he presumed was Agathail. He lifted the box to see how full it was. It was empty. Then he glanced something under the counter that made his heart jump. A voce'angelii.

It was the most beautiful instrument in existence.

Crafted from various crystals and stones. It was polished to perfection into two cylinders, one large enough to fit around an arm with a hole at the bottom and at the top a longer, slimmer cylinder. Both were encrusted with stunning oval cabochon gems, normally of a similar colour to the stone that made the body of the instrument. The bow was made of deer leg bone and the hair was normally unicorn tail hair. To play it, the musician had to bow smoothly up and down the cylinders. This ignited a mysterious light within and cause the stones to sing like ethereal beings. He had only ever seen a voce'angelii once when he was five, on the King's coronation day celebrations and it had forever enchanted him.

"Like what you see?" purred a deep voice in his ear.

Wolflock jerked back and saw a lazy, short haired black cat with giant yellow eyes, watching him.

"Everything has a price," the cat said through its contented purrs.

"Oh really? And how much would the voce'angelii be?"

"That depends."

"On what?"

"On whether or not you can appease her."

The woman came up the counter, rapping her gnarled fingers on the polished wood, Mothy in tow.

"That'll be thirty deimas."

Mothy's face dropped, but Wolflock reached for his satchel.

"How much for the voce'angelii?"

Agathail raised her sharp eyebrow. "You're a snoop."

"I know you've had a hard year too."

"And a thief, now too?"

"Not a thief. Just a snoop."

"It's five thousand deimas."

"What? That's ridiculous!"

Agathail leaned forward, staring at him with the same yellow eyes as her cat.

"Perhaps he could earn it by bringing in some more customers?" the cat said, slinking under her chin. "He's not wrong about your hard year. I told you not to make it storm on that dancer boy's birthday. Just bringing the busking dancers over may turn your fortune for the last of the season."

Agathail glared at her cat and then at Wolflock.

"If you can get a crowd in front of my store, I'll reduce the price of the voce'angelii."

"Deal."

Wolflock saw Mothy bite his lip as he played with the five deimas in his pocket.

"And we get to keep the coins we make from the onlookers."

"You're the ones busking. Go for your lives. Just hang up this medallion as you go."

She handed them a large bronze disc with a sigil carved into it.

"It's for attracting prosperity."

"It's been a while since you used that," the cat purred, rubbing itself against the disc.

Mothy relaxed as Wolflock extended their deal, and they hung up the medallion before following the music to find the dancers. Wolflock and Mothy spotted the curly red-haired dancer from earlier and waved her over to explain the situation. She eyed them both smugly and took them both by the arm.

"Sure. Me and the girls'll help you, but you gotta split the earnings for the hour."

"As long as we get at least twenty-five deimas we'll be happy," Mothy said pointedly.

"Easy. Come on then, join us and we'll move our hips over there!"

Mothy and Wolflock were both given tambourines. They were to stay in the middle of the troop so the girls could grab onlookers and bring them into the dance. Singing, chanting, clapping, and smiling seemed to bring more and more people in. Especially when the red-haired girl danced closely around them, which made it harder for Mothy to catch coins in his baker's hat. They made their way through the streets, directing the crowd to the apothecary. Feet tapping and with a great energy, people started to go into the store. In fact, Wolflock noticed that the store seemed to glow with a very inviting aura. He felt a heavy hat pressed into his hand as Mothy was pulled away to dance with two of the girls. They joined hands and started spinning in a circle that kept growing as more people joined it. Five, six, seven, ten people joined the circle, and it soon got too big for the street. Wolflock stepped inside the awning, still beating his tambourine as the red-haired dancer grabbed Mothy. She pulled him into the middle of the circle, clapping and dancing around him as he tapped his own tambourine. Wolflock saw his cheeks had gone pink with the special attention. The crowd started singing louder and louder. The hat got heavier and heavier with coins.

Wolflock looked around the crowd, seeing all the smiling faces, except one. Mothy played along with the dancer, but he clearly wasn't expecting her to throw her leg around his waist and pull his lips into an embrace.

Neither was Nü.

The crowd cheered loudly, and the dancers bowed

as Mothy pushed the fiery red head away, just in time to see Nü shake her head and run.

The crowd blocked Wolflock, but he saw Mothy shout out to Nü and run after her, leaving Wolflock with the coin-filled hat.

CHAPTER 2

Misadventure on Mabon

Wolflock handed back the tambourine and half of their earnings as promised, staying as taciturn as etiquette would allow.

"If I didn't scare your friend off tell him he should send me word when he's back in town," the redhead smirked. Her giggling troop of dancers seemed very in on some joke between them all. "Also, if you're ever back in town, I have a few friends who like a tall, dark and mysterious man."

"Is that so?" Wolflock muttered, counting out the coins. He gritted his teeth, trying to hold back the torrent of vitriol he wanted to unleash. Mothy wouldn't like it.

"Yea, so you just have to be tall, dark and handsome and she might dance with you." The gaggle of dancers broke out into fits of hysterical laughter. To Wolflock they sounded like asthmatic crows.

Putting his money in his satchel, he scanned the girls, much like they had scanned him earlier. But instead of appraising their desirability, he was looking for other things.

One had heavy make up over pocked skin and she kept touching her face, wiping carefully under her eyes to reshape her flaking eyeliner. Another was shorter and thicker than the others, wearing a tight band around her middle, visible when she pulled at her shirt. One of her hands was guarding her stomach and the other rubbed her chubby arms as she guffawed. The last back up dancer was wearing a skirt of fraying fabric with no shoes and fake gold painted chipped bangles. The lead girl, the red-haired wildling, was the best dressed, but also showed the most about herself. Her hair was tied back with glittering gemstones. Wolflock knew no one actually tied their hair with diamonds, especially in a marketplace where they could be so easily lost. They were fake. As were a few other things.

"Is that so?" Wolflock repeated, his tone smooth

and appeasing. For a moment he would let fly, but then Mothy's upset face at him being unkind flashed before him. Mothy wouldn't approve. He finished putting the coins away and gathered his things.

"Shame he dashed off after that foreign girl. She's not half as pretty as us and he would be such a fun pet."

Wolflock felt a bolt of lightning flash through his mind. She... did not...just... say... that. He thought with a painful clarity. His eyebrow twitched.

"Is that so?" he snarled through a threatening grin.

He was the same height as the young lady, but as he stepped closer, he stood as tall as he could. She grinned back at him as if she thought she was luring him in to set him up for another humiliating fall.

"It's funny you know," he began, digging his nails into his palm, "as the eldest and heir to half the Felen family estate people think that we only know horses. But I know a herd of cattle when I see one."

The red head recoiled, and the other girls stopped their incessant tittering.

"Excuse me?" Red scoffed.

"You aren't excused. See, the women of dignity I know, know how to apply makeup in a way that naturally emphasises their best features. They do not slather it on so thick that it weighs more than their jewellery. Also, only low-quality products cause blemishes I'm told. So, clearly your talentless dancing is not fulfilling your fiscal needs." He rounded from the first to the second. "I also understand that with anything practice makes perfect and judging by how you performed, or rather, didn't perform earlier, I'd say that you should return to your family. You're going to starve on the streets if you rely on some flighty dream you're not prepared to put effort into." The first two had shirked back like cornered mice. To Wolflock's amusement, the one with poor quality attire stood forward like she thought he wouldn't find anything to say to her.

"Just... just no. You're not good at appraising. Can you even read? Just go and get employment in town, for pity's sake. I can tell you were swindled on all your jewellery and you made a poor choice in footwear as all of your companions still have tolerable shoes. You clearly can't tell silk from satin or cotton. Go back to school before you try puffing your chest out as if you've no faults."

"Don't listen to him, girls. He doesn't know anything!" Red fired up, balling her fists and stomping forward.

"Is that so?" Wolflock hissed through a sly smile. "Well, well, well, Miss Red. You, who are the leader of this," he didn't know what to call their troop. He merely waved the back of his hand at them. "Tying your hair up with fake gemstones? Adorning yourself with copper painted as gold? Oh yes, I can see the blue tinge it's left on your skin. Your earrings, bangles and your necklace are all fakes. I'd say the gemstones anywhere on you are coloured glass. Ah and yes," he pinched the fabric of the layers of her skirt, making her jump back, "as I thought. Even fake fabrics. Not even good fakes. This is barely hessian let alone cotton and silk. The thread count is dismal, and the sensation is enough to make you itch. Is that why you have to taunt and prey on travellers passing though? No boy will pay you any significant attention? They probably can't stand to be near you. It's not just your clothing that feels awful to touch, but likely to your personality. Is that why you surround yourself with the sentus-less, the unactionable dreamers, the insecure? You have to surround yourself with those you think are less than you because to be in a room of people who are better than you is terrifying. Far too much effort, am I right? And at your heart you know your greatest sin is apathy, closely followed by arrogance."

The red-haired girl and her troop stayed deathly silent.

"Oh? Did I miss out that your family are criminals? The only reason you have these possessions is not through an ignorant transaction. Oh no, but rather because your kin counterfeited them. As is evident by the consistent brand of the insignia P.F. on each visible piece."

Wolflock expected the rage in her eyes. He expected the others to back away as they did. He did not expect the wind to whip around her and for her hands to burst into flame.

"You're dead meat, Felen."

Wolflock's eyes went wide and he stepped back, nearly falling on the stairs, but he felt someone behind him.

"Sica, that's enough. Be gone from my store and be gone with that flame." Agathail waved her hand over Wolflock's shoulder and rain began pouring down from a clear blue sky.

The red-haired girl snarled, turned on her heel and stormed away with her friends scurrying behind her. They whispered and glared back over their shoulders until they were out of sight.

"Didn't know you had the magic of sight," Agathail hummed, impressed.

"No. It's the power of deduction. It's rather simple. Umm... here." He gave her the coins for Mothy's gifts. "Can you send it all up to the Silver Ice Hair? And wrap them in something nice. I'm not in the mood to have him wrangle me into more chores."

Agathail shrugged. "Sure. This is a thing I can do. You two are like brothers, I see. You did him a kindness and in return you may have made a dangerous enemy."

It was Wolflock's turn to shrug. "That's nothing new. You should hear what I did in my hometown."

He didn't speak with Agathail for much longer before making his way back to the ship. He wasn't ready to go back onto the silvery grey ship yet, but he also didn't want to spend any more time in the markets. Instead, he wandered up and down the docks, watching the comings and goings of the surrounding life.

Dock workers were out in droves. They shouted at one another, shooed gulls off fish drying on racks, and flirted with the passengers loitering around the dock. Some children were fishing off the piers. Others were chasing off the river gulls, squealing as they came too close to the water. A pair of what Wolflock assumed were 'local' boys tried to push each other into the water but both ended up toppling in. Cattle, sheep and goats milled around eating the grass behind the stalls, too dull to know they were to be sold. Even a dog was trotting back and forth, scavenging scraps wherever it could find them.

It was all so peaceful... on the surface.

Wolflock could see that each dock worker had

different tattoos, some rather sinister, such as blades, skulls or gory images. There were clear rankings in their workplace hierarchy that weren't always appreciated. Several workers were jovial to their superior's faces, but the moment their backs were turned, would scoff, scowl and make rude gestures. Wolflock even saw one of them pocket something out of a crate he was meant to be moving.

The children had a similar hierarchy, but it was based on age, then size. None of them were wearing shoes, and they all looked a little too spindly. Homeless. Or orphans judging by their pure pack-like manners.

Runaways, Wolflock concluded.

Thought they'd join a circus or go and become a performer at the markets and couldn't find their way home when their bellies started aching. The dog was skinny too. It snarled whenever anyone came near it.

It's a stray.

Its tail wagging appeared to be more from anxiety than happiness. The livestock seemed to be the only creatures that were truly calm and content. Even if it was only before they were to be separated and sold.

Wolflock spied a familiar face amongst the throng of people before him. Yifi was biting a plump lip, looking around with an anxious stare. Her honey brown hair cascaded around her shoulders and her darting eyes looked hazel in the sunlight. She stood between a large dock worker and a stack of crates.

"Please, sir," she pleaded, "it's fine. I will wait for my friends to-"

"Nonsense," the gruff man growled, "Lemme 'elp yah get these to yah room. Pretty little thing like you might get a splinta."

"Miss Voof, merry meet," Wolflock interjected. "I see you need assistance with your belongings. Shall I call the Captain and First Mate to assist? I'm sure it'll be easier."

"Now listen 'ere you..."

"Sorry, good sir. I thought I'd save you the paperwork. We've recently had an outbreak on the ship of some mysterious disease and quarantine has been a nightmare. Best let the right people handle the right job, am I right?"

Only standing five and a half feet tall, and being one third the large man's width, Wolflock was not physically imposing in the slightest. He knew how to do the bureaucratic tango, though. He also knew how vehemently tradesfolk and labourers despised it.

"Sick? Ah... not to worry then. I'm sure your people 'ave it all in hand. Merry part." The thick man slumped off, disappointed.

Yifi sighed, drawing her hood further over her face. Wolflock noticed she was wearing a bracelet of woven fishing line with little pretty lures hanging from it. "Thank you, Wolflock. I appreciate it. Oh! Here! Take this as thanks."

She dug through one of her three large crates and handed him a pink heart card with white lace.

"Ah... Yifi? I don't think you meant this for me..."

"Oh! Oh my, ha. That would have been a shock." She snatched back the card and tore it up. "Umm... how about this!"

She flung a cardboard box into his hands with a little tag attached saying, 'So you finally write me back'.

"What is this?" Wolflock asked as he pried the lid open.

"It's... umm... well you'll just have to open it and find out," she huffed, peeking into it to see what it was.

It was filled with beautiful stationary. A fresh fountain pen, a black ink pot filled and corked, elegantly bordered envelopes and blank pages. There was also a golden paperweight with Yifi's initials monogrammed into it. Wolflock picked up a rosewood handled magnifying glass. As he examined it, he also spied a letter opener with the same rosewood handle and a pretty letter sealing kit.

"Happy Mabon, Mr Felen. My life is more often improved by your presence than it is diminished. For that I am grateful."

Wolflock thought the stationery kit was handsome. Enough so, that he didn't feel too awkward about Yifi expressing her gratitude. "Thank you. What is all this though?" he gestured to the crates.

Yifi opened her mouth to answer but stopped as she spied someone over Wolflock's shoulder. Her smile radiated warmth for a moment, but it vanished as she turned to lock the crates again.

"Miss Voof!" Slavidus called. Wolflock turned to see he held two little bags in his right hand. "Miss Voof, I'm glad I caught you. Merry meet, Wolflock." He went to continue speaking, but eyed Wolflock again before refraining.

"Yifi needs help getting her things on board." Wolflock folded his arms, disgruntled at not being more privy to Slavidus' intended conversation. He scanned the first mate. He had a lump in his back pocket smaller than a pocket watch but larger than a locket. The two bags he held were tied with a cute ribbon that Wolflock had seen earlier at a confectionary stall. He didn't know what was in the back pocket, but he knew Slavidus didn't want to share his treats with anyone but Yifi.

"Aye. And a good thing to want to," he mumbled as he and Yifi smiled at one another. Wolflock tapped his foot and scoffed at the saccharine display. Slavidus shook his head and waved to Geagle, who was holding the cargo logbook close to his side. "Geagle! Come help Mr Felen take Miss Voof's things to the hull. There's a good lad. Shall we away for a late lunch?" he held out his arm for Yifi to take.

"But-I-Slav-No!"

But they had already walked into the crowd of people watching a juggler on the dock and couldn't hear his protestations.

"If you just-"

"I know how to lift a box!" Wolflock snapped, dipping down and using his back to lift. Geagle had placed the ship's cargo log on top. It was a plain brown book with the starting date pyrographed into the cover and spine. Wolflock thought it was odd that Geagle would have it so close to him.

Perhaps he's lost it in the past and is being cautious.

"These boxes are pretty light," the thin-haired man chortled. Wolflock felt his arms straining.

They got it into the hull and Wolflock panted.

"Are you well, Mr Wolflock?"

"Fine. I'm... Not one for lifting boxes like this."

"Well... ah... I'll go get the rest. They is pretty light for me."

Wolflock nodded, unable to speak further.

As Geagle left, Wolflock glanced around. The hull was fuller than he'd seen it. Bags of grains, barrels of vegetables and crates of goodness knows what else filled the room to where it was claustrophobic. He took a moment to look at who had received good besides Yifi. Nan Ji had a few more boxes of herbs. Froderyk and Fuhji had some intricate trunks, most likely with Fuhji's returned belongings. Stra had three new nondescript chests. Veluse had a new box with fresh paints, and Dlumi had a small bundle of letters.

Wolflock took the letter opener from the stationary Yifi had given him and began unwinding the screws on the lock. Yifi had wanted to hide this, and he wanted to know why. Before he could finish, Geagle came down with the last two boxes.

"Thanks for waiting, Mr Wolflock."

Wolflock sighed and pretended to help him lower the boxes.

"That's about the last of it. Best yeh be going upstairs now."

"I'm fine down here thanks. It's nice and quiet."

Geagle bit his lip, looking everywhere except at

Wolflock. "I... umm... I can't leave yeh down here alone. Captain doesn't like that."

"I'm sure he'll be fine with it. He normally lets Mothy and I stay down here."

"I... umm... I," Geagle shuffled from one foot to the other, "I can't..."

"Wolflock? What in blue blazes are yeh doin' down there! Geagle don' listen to 'im," Grogen stomped down the stairs and clapped Geagle on the shoulder. "He's up to mischief. C'mon, you. You're 'elping me hang up decorations."

Wolflock groaned. "I was just having fun."

"All a'yeh get outta 'ere. C'mon," Grogen waved again, waiting for both younger men to relocate.

Wolflock started to make his way to his room, but Grogen grabbed him by the back of his collar.

"Oh no yeh don't."

"You weren't serious about me helping, were you?"

"O' course I was. Your idle hands are far more dangerous than the mischief yeh can get up to under me nose. Upstairs with yeh."

Wolflock proceeded to grumble and complain for the next few hours. He was forced to hang up strings of sticky cords from the central mast, around the taffrails and let the rest trail in the water. They were soaked in a liquid meant to attract a particular type of glowing river insect. He hung streamers of paper leaves between the sticky cords like a spider web. The goods the passengers purchased while ashore were delivered, including Mothy's Mabon gifts for everyone. As he was hanging ribbons of gold, red and orange around the wreaths of wheat Grogen had hung around the dining hall, Mothy came back on board. Wolflock noted that his shoulders were slumped, and his expression was distant.

"Things didn't go well?" he asked as Mothy made his way towards the dining hall.

"I couldn't find her. I really wanted to apologise."

"You'll get your chance," Wolflock shrugged. "And if she still says no then we're only going to be on the ship for a month more, then you'll never have to see her again."

Mothy frowned in thought, shook his head and pushed passed into the dining hall. Wolflock looked back at Grogen, who rolled his eyes.

"Go on then. I'll catch yeh for clean up tomorrow."

The rest of the crew and company came on board, but Nan Ji ushered his children downstairs before Mothy could catch Nü.

"Let's go and watch the launch. I know a pretty good spot," Wolflock grinned as Mothy passed him a tea.

"Sure. Sounds good," he sighed.

Grogen came back to the kitchen and soon the scrumptious smells of pumpkin, pastries, and baked citrus followed them, even as they climbed the rigging to the crow's nest. Cinnamon, nutmeg, cardamom and aniseed incenses and tea were being passed out below to everyone. The Silver Ice Hair's pristine white sails dropped, the ornate anchor weighed, and the captain shouted orders to the crew as they organised to sail. Wolflock had seen them at it for weeks now, so he had a good idea of what each did. The excitement of the launch and pulling away from the Krieger Zwerg Watchtower brought a smile back to Mothy's face. They both agreed it had been nice to have solid ground underfoot for a few hours. They also agreed that being back on the ship brought a sense of relief. The game began below as the feast was prepared. A few of the passengers were carrying around brown bottles that Wolflock hadn't seen on the ship before. He figured that they must be part of the new cargo.

The children ran around pretending to fly on brooms, jumping over shortly stacked poles. Nan Ji chased his son's around with one of the brown bottles and looked happier than Wolflock had ever seen him. Some of the adults tried walking across a balancing beam, laughing as they toppled off, especially when Froderyk fell three times in a row.

Mothy watched dolefully as Nü tried to beat Slavidus' time for a game where you swept marbles into a bucket. Parihaan couldn't seem to get a single one in, but she seemed to think it was hilarious and Yifi giggled with her. Wolflock got sick of his friend's moping and dragged him downstairs as the sun set. Twelve hours of daylight had passed them, and now twelve hours of night lay ahead.

They joined in on a game where the winner had to dehusk five corn cobs the fastest, which Hognut won every single time. Mothy claimed that his pipe gave him the ability to strip the husk off a corn in the blink of an eye.

The Captain had secured a particularly fat sheep to roast, as well as for the wool to be spun by whoever was interested. The smell of rosemary, garlic, and lamb tantalised the nostrils of every single person on the ship. Before the feast could begin, the captain wanted everyone to gather on the deck with a lantern. Slavidus took the helm as the captain called for the entire company to snuff their lights.

The ship plunged into darkness and all Wolflock could hear was the slosh of water against the ship. Then, very slowly, gold, white and orange lights started to climb up the sticky cords he'd tied earlier. Tiny river grubs inched their way to the mast, gently illuminating the ship in their twinkling light. The sight was beautiful. Wolflock looked to see Mothy's face, but he was looking at Nü.

"And now, company of the Silver Ice Hair, I welcome you to join us under the magic of the night to the Mabon feast."

The crowd cheered and went inside the dining hall to a stunning sight. Through the windows they could see the glittering streams, giving the room a sparkling effect. The crew had tied ribbons from the central candelabra to the walls, making the ceiling look like the underneath of a giant apple. The two long tables had been pushed together to form one big banquet table and bundles of gifts laid over a trestle table to the side. Wolflock felt a pang of guilt and he hoped that no one got him anything.

They took their seats, Wolflock sat at the far end next to Mothy, with Veluse on one side and Tanni on the other. His gut twisted. The full-bodied smells flooding his nostrils made him hungry, but those memories of being made to eat more than he wanted to also came flooding back. Something was different though. The people around the table were talking, laughing, and picking at the grapes and nuts laid out. His family would have spoken quietly to each other, gossiping and making suspicious eyes at him. He was jerked back to the present by Froderyk shouting at the other end of the table to Hognut who was sitting two seats away from Mothy. Grogen was tuning his guitar by the Captain and Haatji had a drum she was tapping now and then.

Perhaps this will be different.

Captain Blutro stood up, tapping his knife against a special silver goblet.

"Welcome, everyone. As is Mabon custom, we all have to stare at this amazing food for another half an hour before we can tuck in. But we hold ourselves back for an important reason. To honour the earth, the farms, the forests, the sky, and especially the river, we sacrifice a little time and give thanks for this year gone. So, let's go around the table and give thanks for our most special thing or things in the past year. I'll go first. I am thankful for my delightful crew of rag-tag scoundrels-"

The crew around the table cheered and clapped, hooting loudly. Geagle seemed to make a bit more noise than was necessary.

"-And of course, I'm grateful to our protector and guide, Houl. May his blessings continue until I can thank him again next year."

The Captain sat down and Slavidus rose. Wolflock saw him fiddling with something in his back pocket.

"I can never top your speeches, Captain. I am..." he looked at Yifi and blushed, "I am grateful for... being able to be your loyal first mate. May we continue to have Houl's blessings and our adventures." He finished quickly and sat down, avoiding Yifi's troubled eyes.

Grogen stood up next and strummed his guitar. "I'm grateful for me angelic voice." Everyone laughed as he made it as rough and gruff as he could, but he strummed a few chords for the company and sat back down as they applauded.

Froderyk and Fuhji stood up together, which seemed to be necessary as Froderyk wobbled on the spot.

"I am so happy-" Froderyk hiccupped.

"We are so happy we can be honest with you all. We've made such good friends and we hope that we'll stay friends when we finish our journey," Fuhji interrupted him and tugged him back into his seat.

"Yes!" he burped. "That."

Wolflock glanced around the table at the responses to the odd behaviour. The Captain looked furious, Slavidus looked confused, but Yifi, Nan Ji and Geagle looked away. Parihaan's expression was odd. As if it were a mixture of amusement and concern.

Nan Ji stood up next, followed by Nü, Gege and Didi.

"We call this festival Qiūfēn in Shrùikèn. I," he slurred, "Am grateful I even have children in the first place! Who would have thought such a pretty wife would have chosen me? I am grateful for the time I spent with her."

He sat back down clumsily and rolled a brown bottle in his hands.

Nü stood like a marble statue, not making eye contact with anyone. "I am grateful for my family and friends."

"I am grateful for my father," both of her brother's said, causing silent tears to roll down their father's cheeks.

Matroos, a crewman from Quarenth stood and said he was thankful for the river and the new shoes the Captain had gotten him for his birthday. It made Wolflock's gut turn. It sounded like Myna. What was he thankful for? For once in his life he could say things that meant something to him, but it was foolish. All the answers going through his head were nonsense.

Parihaan rose, blushing as she glanced around.

"I'm grateful that the folks on this ship can still make a lady feel loved."

Geagle helped her down and took his turn. "I'm grateful for all the love in my life!"

His ears turned bright red and Wolflock saw the Captain had been watching everyone carefully. They caught each other's eye knowingly before continuing to observe the room.

Haatji giggled next to him, standing up and glancing about the room from behind her translucent orange veil. "I'm grateful for new experiences and new friends."

Wolflock couldn't help but notice that she slurred when she projected her voice across the table.

"I'm grateful to have the most charming and inspiring company to paint," Veluse smiled with a great flourishing of hands.

Wolflock's gut clenched. It was his turn. He stood up slowly, trying to think of what to say.

"I..." he mumbled, looking at Mothy's sad eyes. "I..." The Captain looked at him with the same stern look his father would look at him with. He felt his knees crumble. "I... I'm grateful for my writing implements, the fairy dust lanterns and the ship's giant cooking pot." Wolflock felt all their eyes burning into him. It was just like his aunts and cousins. A mixture of anger, embarrassment and defiance filled his chest, and he felt his face grow red. "I'm grateful for this silly festival to be over."

He couldn't sit. He couldn't stay. He couldn't breathe.

Without another word he stood up and stalked to the door with his shoulders hunched up to his ears. He couldn't. He couldn't say what he really wanted to say. They'd all judge him, and he'd worked so hard to be liked lately. They'd desert him and ostracise him. He'd be alone again and have to retreat away for another month while they sailed away. He could see it all now and his gut twisted into knots at the thought.

Wolflock felt the sting of the cold Autumn air on his face and hands and realised he was holding his breath. He exhaled fog as he moved to the front of the ship, gripping the railing and closing his eyes to clear his mind.

He'd only felt this once before when his father enrolled him into the local school after the men abducted his mother. It was during the Mabon celebration that he'd said he was grateful for his new chemistry set. All his other classmates started avoiding him because he was wealthier than them. They made fun of him for not saying he was grateful for the friends he'd made. Stupid jokes circulated about him being a chemistry set, whatever that meant, and he went home crying. His father soon organised a private tutor, and he didn't have to see those classmates ever again.

He could see it all happening again though. He'd be honest and he'd be left alone again, but this time he actually liked the people around him. He'd worked hard to make friends.

Perhaps that is the problem...

He had started to care.

He shook his head, his black hair blowing back into

place from his face as the ship sliced through the glittering dark water below. As he exhaled, he knew he'd had to nip that in the bud. He'd have to work on it to make sure he went back to seeing the other people on board as specimens and scientific examples. It would certainly make him feel safer. Then he'd be able to play along but remain unscathed by their negative opinions. He'd think far more clearly without all those messy and irrational emotions clouding his mind.

Music exploded from the dining hall along with raucous cheering and song. It was loud enough to snap Wolflock from his thoughts. Some of the voices shouted something about dancing under the stars, so he thought it best to move away. The last thing he wanted was to explain himself to anyone.

As he made his way down to his cabin, he made up his mind.

He would not have any longer friends. He would not try. It was too complicated.

He closed his door and went to bed, pretending to sleep for hours as the party carried on upstairs. It all went quiet in the late hours of the night as people began moving to their cabins. Wolflock heard his door open and, thinking it was Mothy, continued to pretend to sleep. The intruder, who was much larger than Mothy, came in, closed the door and sat on the edge of his bed, sighing.

It's Dlumi or a crew member, he thought.

Wolflock heard them run their fingers over their head and huff in frustration. Just as he was about to roll over and tell them off for being there, the person spoke.

"Are you up, Mr Felen?" Captain Blutro whispered.

Wolflock rolled over and sat up, wide awake. Why was the captain in his room?

"Someone has done something."

"What are you saying, Captain?"

"I'm saying I have a crime I need solved and you're the only one I trust to find it out."

CHAPTER 3
Shards of Proof

"Captain?"

Captain Blutro Silk sighed through his nose as his ponytail purred. The snuffle, Aujin, was quite happy being half tucked in the captain's collar, his moonbeam tail swishing back and forth across the captain's shoulders. "Someone has brought contraband on my ship. I know not who, why nor how. This is what I want you to discover."

"What contraband? I wasn't told of anything I couldn't bring on board when I was researching the ship."

"You're a lad of fifteen Winters. What contraband were you to bring on board my vessel? No. I only say this to passengers who are of age and wanting to bring more than normal luggage."

"So, what is it you'd have me search for?"

"Alcohol."

Wolflock frowned. "But, Captain, I thought alcohol was allowed on the ship. Nan Ji-"

"Uses it for medical cleansing. I'm aware. And that is permitted on my vessel. No. I'm talking about drinking alcohol. Last night, several of the passengers and even one of my crew had consumed it to the point they were ill and unfit to perform their duties. That is inexcusable."

Wolflock watched the older man carefully. His hands were white-knuckled and shaking with the force he held in his fists, and, although he tried to sound calm, his throat was tight, making his words clipped.

"Who has done that?"

Captain Blutro sighed again, looking away. "Geagle. Poor lad. Poor, influenceable lad."

"I can't say I know much about alcohol, Captain. The upper echelon of Plugh and Corl sometimes indulged, but I never saw more than a glass of intricately delicate wine be served. I heard that some establishments were dedicated to the consumption of lesser substances, but I'm not even sure what I'm looking for."

"This." Captain Blutro drew out a napkin and laid it

on Wolflock's desk. It was filled with dark brown glass shards. "This was what I found next to Geagle this morning. He'd fallen asleep on deck. Mr Felen, if my crew are getting drunk, it needs to be stopped for the safety of all. If the passengers are distributing this hateful liquid around, then be prepared for brawls, heated verbal boxing matches and illness to wash over this ship in torrents. We must stop it at the source. At all costs."

"Why not just confront those you find with this bottle, then?"

"When it comes to substances like drinking alcohol, you need to discover who has done this and where they are hiding it before you act. Once people think something they like will be outlawed, they drive it underground. The last thing I need on my honourable vessel is a black market filled with lies. No, lad. We must be subtle and indirect. If the wrong people know we are looking for them, then they'll burrow down like a tick."

Wolflock pulled his blanket back and moved to the brown shards, carefully placing them together.

"I'll need glue. Have you any?"

"I'll get you some from my office. Thank you, Mr Felen. I knew I could count on you."

The Captain returned shortly after with a pot of glue, which Wolflock set to work with by his freshly shaken fairy dust lantern. Piece by piece, shard by shard, edge by edge, he meticulously sealed the glass back together. He knew that most makers had special seals imprinted on their bottles, so if he could put the pieces together and see it, he'd have an important clue. Some were around the body, some collared the neck, and others stamped into the thickest part of the glass. The bottom. He was also wary that some bottles were repurposed and had no sign of their origin.

As he worked into the dawn, he thought to himself how opulence and wealth often lead to more distinct and easier to find markings than those of the common folk. Were his family to ever produce distilled liquids, he could see that his father would create every bottle with a bold neck and body, and a base stamp. This bottle, though, was cheap. Nothing was around the dark amber neck. Turning the newly formed neck he could see that the glass was poorly made, with flecks of dirt and sand still running through it. The dark glass itself was another sign that it was rough craftsmanship. Getting a crystal-clear translucency was a sign of a great glass worker. The rim had a hastily crafted look with a tiny jagged seam that had chunks of the original cork caught on it. The body was bland and round, showing him that the bottle could hold a little more than a pint, but little else.

As the rising sun streamed through his window, making the gritty imperfections of the half melted sand in the shards sparkle, Wolflock put the last pieces of the base together. Again, a sharp seam encircled the thick glass, but he could clearly make out a symbol of an eye with a cross through the pupil. He had never seen it before, but at least now he'd have an idea of what else to look for.

He stretched back just as someone knocked on the door.

"Come in," he hummed.

Mothy entered, wiping his eyes. "You alright?" he yawned.

"Yes? Why wouldn't I be? Here, take a look at this. Have you seen it before?"

Mothy slouched over and examined the bottle. "Yeah. It's a bottle. Lots'a people have them. Why d'you glue this one back together? Don't we have more? You sure you're alright?"

"The Captain asked me to look into who brought this on board and how. But we have to be discreet."

"But... it's a bottle."

"I know it's a bottle, Mothy! It was what was in the bottle that mattered."

"And what was that?"

Wolflock lowered his voice. "Alcohol for drinking."

Mothy made a face. "Yuck. I don't know how anyone can drink that stuff. It tastes awful."

"I have only ever had a small glass of wine, but I agree. It was very tart. The question is, where do we begin?"

Mothy started going through Wolflock's wardrobe, picking out one of his plainer blue vests, a black shirt and freshly pressed slacks. "You know I'm not good to you until I've had food. Let's start at breakfast."

Wolflock nodded, got dressed and walked with Mothy to the dining hall. They were the first ones there besides a few of the night shift crew finishing up for the day. Wolflock collected some toast with purple cliffberry marmalade. Mothy returned with porridge, a bowl of fresh fruit, another of dried fruit, two eggs, two slices of toast, a grilled tomato and fried potato chunks.

Wolflock couldn't help but grin. This was perfect. Mothy would go back for seconds and, if he kept him talking, he could observe all the other passengers. That way he'd see what state they were all in. The ones who were looking particularly worse for wear would be his suspects.

"So, Mothy. Tell me what you know about the other passengers. I'd like to get an idea of what kind of trading and occupation our companions enjoy."

Mothy began rambling right away, occasionally

stopping to take a mouthful of food. He started with the crew members around them, only listening for the key words from Mothy's conversation. Observing them while they ate their breakfast-dinner, Wolflock saw a few things of interest, but not of any consequence. The second engineer on board, Malumi, was broad shouldered and burly. But Wolflock saw that she frequently ran her stubby fingers along the arm of her chair or in the air with surprising agility.

She plays piano, or at least wants to.

Kolor, one of the bosun mates, was bald, as white as a ghost with dark red eyes. It could have been from all the night shift, but she didn't look as tired as the other workers. Wolflock saw her eating bleu steak for breakfast before she put on a broad sunhat to leave.

Vampire? No. She's eating food. Half vampire then.

Groger, the tallest of the crew, looked dead tired. His long blonde hair was wavy and unbraided over his shoulders, tangling with his beard. His normally bulging blue eyes were closed as he nursed a cup of tea on the table, dozing off.

Coming up to his days off soon by the looks of things.

Tanni and her young daughter Tinni were the first to come into breakfast. Bright, sweet and getting happier as each day passed, they said their good mornings before getting their food and talking about the day they expected to have. They were both playing with a beautiful porcelain faced doll that looked strangely like Yifi. Wolflock also saw that Tanni was wearing a new bright blue jewel around her neck.

Gifts from last night? From whom is the real question. They were expensive gifts.

Stra came in not long after, looking sour. He was wearing a mismatched sailor's cap that looked like it was better suited to a stage show. As the door closed behind him, he snatched it off and crammed it into his pocket.

Does he always look that displeased? Wolflock thought as he toyed with his spoon.

Stra was a taller gentleman, but not too tall. Sinewy, but not spindly. His hair was shorn only millimetres from his scalp and his dark brown eyes had odd flecks of mustard yellow through them. Although he was only in his mid to late third decade, his face was lined with scowl marks and creases from frowning. Wolflock knew him as a botanist, but not much else. Until now.

As he grabbed his tea and porridge bowl, Wolflock noted yellow stains on his fingers. Index and middle. *A smoker, but not pipes. He rolls them.*

His nails were stained green. Wolflock knew he

hadn't headed off the ship though, so he deduced he'd been playing with fresh herbs over the last day or so. Perhaps someone brought him something back from their stop. His attire was average. Not poor or ill fitted, but store bought. Not tailored. His tidy button-up shirt had a crease in it where he'd recently taken it out of the packaging and his jacket was oversized. He may have lost a lot of weight at some stage.

"Lockie!" Mothy had stopped chattering. "Lockie look! Its Geagle."

Wolflock's eyes darted around to see the wispy blonde-haired man stagger into the dining hall. One hand on his stomach, the other was rubbing his red eyes. He looked peaky. Wolflock saw him walk in a crooked line to the kitchen space, hands shaking as he put a pot on to boil.

"Not what I expected. Is this normal for when people overindulge in alcohol?" Wolflock's eyes narrowed as he watched the large crewman.

Mothy's lips stretched into an uncomfortable grimace. "Aye. T'is. Sometimes. Shaking, red faced, red-nosed, hot tempered sometimes. Pale, weak and whiny, other times. Sometimes they don't even get out of bed. Just groan 'bout how they're going to die. Then they do it all over again the next night." His words were clipped and the way he listed the symptoms he was aware of gave Wolflock the impression this was a sensitive topic for his friend.

"But why? The side effects hardly look like they're worth any punishment this severe."

Mothy shrugged and was about to offer an answer when Nan Ji and Slavidus stormed in.

"No! No, I will not pay for this. You will take this off my charges. It is not acceptable!" Nan Ji roared, waving a cup under Slavidus' nose.

"Mr Nan!" he pushed the cup away. "For the last time, the cup is not damaged. No one gave you or your children damaged dishes. I just need you to check Geagle's health!"

"I will go to the captain with this!"

"The captain is-"

"And this food! See? It is burnt! Burnt! How can you serve this slop?! My family has scarcely bitten any of the food provided. This will also come off my bill!"

Slavidus looked around wide eyed, shocked at the accusations.

Nan Ji moved to Geagle, who was supporting himself on the bench, one hand over his ears to block the noise. The Xiayahn doctor tore his hand away and inspected the crewman. After a moment of him muttering about the quality of the voyage as he took Geagle's pulse and looked at his tongue, Nan Ji pushed a bag of herbs into his hands.

"Take this. He needs sleep. This will make him sleep until his next shift. That is all. I will have to charge extra for these herbs. Very expensive!"

"You-but-they were pre-packaged!" Slavidus stammered. But Nan Ji had his nose at bench level and was looking for dirt and dust on the kitchen counters.

"And this!" Nan Ji shouted in triumph, snatching up one of the silver goblets used during the Mabon celebrations. "See!? It is rough! We have been drinking metal shards. This will also come off my bill!"

Slavidus pinched the bridge of his pointed nose, closing his eyes as he gripped the thing in his back pocket. "Mr Nan, should you have any grievances with the service aboard this vessel I suggest you write them in Puinteylien and I will-"

"I will have to pay for a translator! That will also come off my bill!" The dark-haired man raised the goblet again, making it sparkle as his hand shook, and stomped out of the dining hall. As he passed Wolflock, he saw that he was still wearing last night's clothes, and they had a familiar acrid odour to them. They could still hear him ranting about things outside.

"-I will shove them in your ears," Slavidus muttered darkly. He caught the boys' eyes and heaved a heavy sigh.

"Sorry lads. Go back to your breakfast. I think the festivities of last night have made him unnecessarily excited..."

The first mate departed after the complaining customer and Wolflock whipped around to Mothy. "Did you see that?"

"Aye... Not pleasant. Poor Slavidus. I wonder what's in Nan Ji's bonnet."

Wolflock blinked. "You didn't see it?"

"I thought we just clarified that I did. The whole room did."

"No, Mothy. Nan Ji. He was trembling."

"He didn't seem that mad. Just... normal mad."

"I know. I think there's more to our favourite doctor's father than he wants us to see. We should start there."

"But isn't Geagle a better option right now? He's the one that was caught being drunk."

"Ah, but he's about to be put into an incapacitated sleep. We'll have to wait for him to wake up this afternoon. I do not believe him to be the mastermind in all this though. He's slow and goes along with others to appease them. When I was writing letters for him, I had to rewrite his 'break-up' letters to two ladies he loved five times because the wording was too severe for him. He would not conduct this act of rule breaking unless it was to appease another on board. Let's consider those possibilities:

Firstly, Geagle was the one found drunk with the broken bottle. We will have to locate the other bottles and those who have them to find their source, but I can see by your expression you are wondering how we may find these individuals. Simple deduction and data collection.

Many people were not acting themselves over the last day besides Geagle. We both saw Slavidus in the forest talking about doing something the captain wouldn't allow. He's also had something in his back pocket ever since the post office."

"Maybe it's a key? Or a ring for Yifi? They've been getting very close lately."

"It is possible, but without data, we only have speculation. Secondly, during the Mabon festival, several people were slurring and struggling to stand. I took note that their actions worried the captain. They were Froderyk, Nan Ji, Haatji and Geagle."

"I thought something was off. Especially with Froderyk!"

"So now we gather data, but we must do so discreetly. Otherwise, the captain has informed me that things will get far more difficult."

"Who do we start with?"

"All of them."

Rhiannon D. Elton

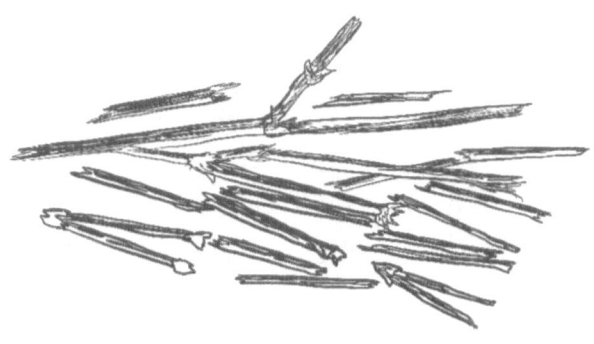

CHAPTER 4

The Mysterious Giver

Wolflock didn't answer Mothy as he asked how they would analyse all the suspects. He sat back with folded his arms and glared at the door as he waited. His breakfast half finished, Wolflock waited. While he was distracted Mothy polished both bowls off, sneaking Wolflock's food away.

He could still hear Nan Ji shouting at Slavidus and the other crew members. He had to wait for that one voice. He scrunched up his face, scowling that he hadn't thought to ask Captain Blutro earlier about getting access to the logs. Now he'd have to wait until Slavidus broke under

Nan Ji's verbal thrashing, go and get the captain to make some form of tentative amends, and then ask him privately. If he didn't wait, he knew they'd be interrupted, and if anyone caught him going through the cargo logs again, people may actually think of him as a thief.

Wolflock shook the thought out of his head. *No. I don't care what they think. They'll prevent me from finding the truth. That's it.*

Mothy said good morning to the Corsh businesswoman Dlumi, the purple and orange twins, Faleen and Bleen, and Parihaan as they came in. Each held some kind of parcel with various cards. Some heart shaped, others pink or red. Even wrapped, Wolflock could spot a chocolate tin under Dlumi's arm. Faleen and Bleen both unwrapped glittering broaches meant for a sophisticated woman, and Parihaan gushed over a pretty new pearl hair comb.

Wolflock eyed Parihaan closely. She wasn't shaking as she put the comb in her thick black hair... She had broken capillaries around her hooked nose and her eyes were tinged yellow, but she was standing fine. Wolflock wondered if she had been drunk at all last night or if she was just naturally clumsy. She looked happier than he'd ever seen her. She'd certainly become more social than she had been before Mabon. She didn't speak about anything intelligent, but she was definitely social.

His thoughts were broken by the sharp silence from downstairs.

"Mothy, let's go."

Mothy grabbed a muffin as Wolflock hauled him out. As they headed downstairs, they saw a many of the doors open as most people had moved onto the deck for a morning stroll before breakfast or were washing in their basins. Wolflock could hear the splash of water or the curse of a gentleman shaving as the ship bobbed. But no yelling from Nan Ji.

The boys saw the Nan children eating a rice and vegetable dish quietly in their room. The three of them had strange parcels with various shades of pink letters and odd trinkets, clearly made for a lady. Mothy stopped, his eyes pleading as he looked at Nü. Wolflock could see she knew he was there, but she refused to turn her gaze.

"Come on, Mothy. We don't have time."

He pulled his sorrowful friend to the Captain's room and pressed his ear to the elegant pale grey wood door. The captain's room was, by far, the nicest on the ship. Wolflock recalled the silver inlaid filigree of dolphins, mermaids and fish throughout the walls inside, but the outer door was like all the others. It was a soft light wood with grey streaks through it, with a silvery swirling lever handle in the shape of a wave, set into an intricately designed backplate. The captain normally left his key in the door, but, ever since Wolflock and Mothy had pushed it through to read through his library four days ago, he had kept it in his desk drawer. Wolflock was aware that Captain Blutro didn't know he knew where the key was kept, but it did make listening at the door easier with the clear opening.

"Fear not, Mr Nan. I will personally review these grievances myself and we shall see to it that your stay on the Silver Ice Hair is to your liking." Captain Blutro spoke with a calm stern tone that seemed to make Nan Ji relax a bit more.

"Very good, Captain. As long as I can get these issues taken off my bill I will be satisfied."

"I'm sure we will come to an arrangement. Fear not, Mr Nan. Silver is the colour of peace and I am confident we will achieve it."

Wolflock looked up at Mothy and they jumped up, backs to the wall on either side of the door as Nan Ji came out. The old man looked calmer, but still grouchy. Wolflock got an even stronger whiff of the acrid odour from earlier. It was what the bottle had smelt like.

If he hasn't been drinking, he's been bathing in the stuff.

Nan Ji walked straight passed them, oblivious to their presence. Wolflock whipped about and they both ducked into the Captain's office. Aujin was eating a baked potato piece on his shoulder as he scratched away at a letter with a fountain quill.

"Mr Felen. Mr Enitnelav. To what do I owe the intrusion?"

"I need to see the logs, Captain. I believe I can narrow down my search with the cargo logs."

Captain Blutro nodded, twirling Aujin's tail. "Aye. Sounds true. Slavidus has them. He said he needed to check a few details. They're in his room presently. I sent him to fetch me some tea. When he returns, I'll keep him here for a few minutes so you may peruse them."

"Thank you, Captain!" Wolflock grinned and whirled back out.

Mothy saluted before following.

"We're hot on our-" Wolflock started to say as they threw open Slavidus door, but he stopped.

Slavidus Oncor was tearing out a page from the very same cargo log they had come to collect.

He looked up like a deer in a spotlight.

"What in the blue blazes are you two doing barging in here?!"

"What in the river God's name are you doing tearing

pages out of a legal document?!" Wolflock retorted just as hotly.

"This isn't none of your business, Mr Felen. Now off with you before I send for the Captain."

Wolflock folded his arms and crossed his legs, leaning against the doorframe. "Go on then. I'll wait."

Slavidus' face flushed crimson, but his clenched fists wrapped around his thumbs and Wolflock knew he'd concede. After his year of being schooled away from home, he had seen many a teacher and student tuck their thumbs into their fists when they lost an argument.

Slavidus drew a breath, bolstering his nerve. "Alright, alright. But it's for a good reason."

"Like hiding who has brought drinking alcohol onto the ship?" Wolflock said sharply.

"What? No! Who-" Slavidus stammered before putting the page back into the thick logbook. "I see... Captain wants you to look for contraband, eh? Well it isn't me. I don't touch the stuff unless its prescribed by the doctor. I... I have less ship related matters."

His hand moved to his pocket.

"Are ya going to propose to Miss Yifi?" Mothy blurted out as Wolflock closed the cabin door.

"What?! N-no. Well... no. No, I... I..."

He sighed and withdrew a long necklace with a palm

sized cushion cut citrine encased in copper lace. It reflected all the light in the room in dazzling rainbow speckles.

"It's an enchanted necklace. It... allows the wearer to show themselves however they want to be perceived."

Mothy scratched his chin, confused, but Wolflock understood.

"Miss Voof is cursed to be irresistibly beautiful. This would give her the freedom to live as she pleases and build the genuine relationships she craves."

"You left before she said what she was grateful for last night..." Slavidus sighed, sitting on the edge of his bed, holding the necklace as if it pained him. "She said... the blind. She was grateful for the blind..."

"Why didn't you give this to her last night?" Mothy asked. Wolflock glared. He already knew the answer.

"He thinks she'd leave him."

Both Mothy and Slavidus stared in alarm at Wolflock's cold tone. "Captain Blutro doesn't allow this level of passenger fraternization on board because he's likely to lose good crew through it. You've played off your love affair as a friendship or as nothing serious, but you specifically ordered this necklace for her. This isn't something that is common, nor is it cheap. A powerful enchantment like this is possibly even black-market material. Now you're hesitating because you're torn. You don't want her to be free of her curse because if she is, then she may choose another. If she is free to choose someone who can also convince her that they love her spirit and not her looks, then why would she choose you? This may be one of the most foolish and selfish things I have ever seen a man do, Slavidus. And I have seen many a terribly selfish deed."

Slavidus broke into sobs, gripping the necklace with all his might. "I know it is. I know. I just... I've never loved a woman this much before and I don't want to be without her. I ordered this for her months ago and I thought it would have missed us. I was just going to give it to her as a parting gift, but it's here and we still have a month of travel left. I didn't think I would feel this way about her. I thought it would have just been... physical. But I love her. I don't care what she looks like. I just want her to be happy..."

"As long as that happiness is with you."

Slavidus wiped his eyes and sighed, "I... I just want to know if she feels the same. Now I'm not so sure. I thought she did. Now that you've come in telling me someone has smuggled booze onto the ship... I'm worried. Yifi got crates of goods on board recently. What if she was getting close to me just to smuggle things more easily? When she got so cagey about me asking what she'd brought back on from Mabon I started to get worried. Bloody Geagle took worthless notes on the cargo. Crates and barrels?! Who does that!?"

"And that is why you were tearing out the page. To confront her with it. It seems our interests may be aligned, First Mate Oncor," Wolflock moved over to the log, smugly staring down at it. "Let me view the log and I will let you know if Yifi's intentions were indeed to manipulate you."

"Or if she's sincere!" Mothy huffed, glaring at Wolflock.

"Or if she is sincere."

"Very well, lads. Captain has said you can, so no point in me stopping you. Maybe you can see something I can't," He said as he wiped his eyes with his sleeve.

Wolflock looked over the large page detailing what had been taken onboard. The register detailed the items, where they were shipped from, where they were being shipped to, and who signed for them.

On the 22nd of Eolas Revari,

Unloaded from the Cargo Hold of the Silver Ice Hair, Captained by Blutro Silk, First Mate Slavidus Oncor:

Half Crate of broken wears, Shellinmerth, Kreiger Zwerg,
Slavidus Oncor
10 Yards of Silk, Corl, Krieger Zwerg, Slavidus Oncor
2 Barrels Tuiti Fruit, North Zilber River, Krieger Zwerg,
Slavidus Oncor
14 Empty Barrels, Shellinmerth, Krieger Zwerg, Slavidus
Oncor
12 Empty Crates, Shellinmerth, Krieger Zwerg, Slavidus
Oncor
2 pairs of trousers, North Zilber River, Krieger Zwerg,
Slavidus Oncor
6 shirts, North Zilber River, Krieger Zwerg, Slavidus
Oncor
3 pairs of shoes, North Zilber River, Krieger Zwerg
Slavidus Oncor

(Note: All clothing is to be given to Seamstress
Fringle for mending to be picked up at midwinter)

Nothing looked particularly out of the ordinary, so
Wolflock moved on to the cargo brought onto the ship.
The first thing he noticed was that the columns were
lined differently. It was lined under the titles: item,
shipped from, shipped to, signed for, and crew initials.
He suspected that the "signed for" column was who was

the intended recipient, and the crew members initials were confirmation they had received it with a witness present.

Loaded into the Cargo Hold of the Silver Ice Hair, Captained by order of Blutro Silk, First Mate Slavidus Oncor:

1 small box (incense), Carnivale Troop Passenger Faleen Quaretz, S.O.
1 small trunk (Personals) Nebralt family   Passenger, Parihaan Nebralt, S.O.
2 trunks of herbs, Yin Hua Clinic Farm,   Passenger, Nan Ji, S.O.
2 textbooks on metals, Dua Restire, 1st Engineer, Umkombe Shariff, S.O.
4 crates of miscellaneous trinkets, As tagged individually, Passenger, Yifi Voof, G.
12 Barrels of water, -, Ship, -
4 crates of food stuffs, -, Ship,   -
1 special wrapped gift, Local vendor, Geagle, Geagle, G.
3 Boxes of papers (Heavy), As tagged individually, Passenger, Froderyk J. Timmerman G.
1 engagement gift, Quathie Felinya, Passenger, Fuhji Korsaki, G.

"Why are these ones for the ship left blank? Why were they loaded on at all? This isn't permitted anywhere in this ledger at all."

"In that you are correct. I believe I saw you and Miss Yifi talking before I collected her at the Krieger Zwerg dock. I left Geagle in charge. He'd been nagging me all day to go ashore but all he did was hang about the dock, so I got him to man the last hour and take care of it. It looks like he forgot to itemise these twelve barrels. Now we don't know which ones they are."

Wolflock scanned the page. Geagle's hard loopy initials marked Yifi's crates, left a gap for the barrels and then resumed for when Froderyk brought his items on board.

"Is Geagle smart enough to smuggle something on?"

"Doubt it. And he's as loyal as they come. Someone must have confused him. Or one of the dock ladies fluttered her eyelashes at him."

"Ah yes..." Wolflock thought back to Haatji flirting with him. That was earlier in the day though and not during the hour the incident occurred. "This will require more digging, but until then, let's have a look at Yifi's things and see if we can solve at least one part of this puzzle."

The boys left Slavidus in his room while they snuck

into the hull, dodging the sleeping night crew and incapacitated Geagle. The dry, dusty hull smelled like wood shavings and sap, with a hint of oil from the polish used on the ship's furniture. Wolflock knew where everyone's belongings were stored as they were typically positioned directly under their rooms on both sides of the hull walls, cordoned off by smooth hemp ropes. The central area, and most accessible, was the storage for the Silver Ice Hair, stacked with hundreds of barrels, boxes and crates. At the stern was a waste management system, and at the rear were emergency building supplies should the ship become excessively damaged.

Wolflock had also made a mental note of who resided in each room. Yifi's belongings were on the mid starboard side of the ship, diagonally across from his own. He saw several trunks and four crates about three feet high and wide. Wolflock tapped on the trunks first, then flicked them open.

She's either very trusting or doesn't care much for these items. He thought, noting the lack of lock.

Clothes. All manner of unworn clothes. Pretty, delicate, fur lined. Clothes of all different colours and styles, some from distant countries. The only thing was a small box filled with love letters. They'd been scrunched up, but Yifi had smoothed them out, laying them neatly in the box. Each was started "To the Lady of my Dreams" and finished with "From the man who would go blind for your love."

Wolflock knew this handwriting. It was the very same he'd seen in the cargo logbook and the ship's roster. Slavidus.

And yet she wears the simplest, plainest clothes of any woman on the ship.

No bottles or alcohol though. Wolflock moved to Mothy who was wiggling open the first crate.

"Most people don't realise that if you wriggle the lid, the lock will act as a hinge and give you enough room to get the bolts free," he huffed and puffed, lifting the solid wood. "And in box number one!"

"Nothing." Wolflock breathed, stunned by the lack of anything in the crate.

"What?"

"It's empty." His brow knitted with confusion.

"You're not serious!" Mothy groaned.

"Was Yifi intoxicated last night?"

Mothy shook his head and huffed as he wriggled the hinge bolts back into place.

Wolflock pinched his chin and glared at the empty box. Suddenly, he drew out his letter opener to finish working on the crate he'd been toying with earlier. He had to know why the box was empty and perhaps the second would yield better results.

"You can just unscrew them too. Yifi isn't particularly security conscious. If anything, I'd say she wasn't attached to these items much at all. These locks have been placed on here by the courier, not her."

Mothy stopped, eyeing Wolflock suspiciously.

"Would you say she was asking for her things to be stolen?"

Wolflock flicked his dark hair out of his face, regretting not oiling it this morning. "Don't be daft, Mothy. The word theft denotes some kind of non-consensual taking of a possession. No one asks to have something stolen. That is the very nature of the word. Look. This one is half empty. No alcohol either. Just... junk"

"I'd say half full."

Wolflock frowned, opening the third. "This is the same."

"Why would Yifi have brought on an empty crate and two half full ones?" Mothy peered quizzically at the pink and pretty knick knacks. "Did she buy all this ashore?"

Wolflock flicked through the various crumpled and torn cards squashed between the items. They were far less cared for than the smoothed out ones in the separate box.

"'To my dearest beloved, please write me back, my heart yearns to see your beautiful face again.' 'To my one true darling, I crave the touch of your beautiful hands in mine.' 'I could stare into your eyes for all eternity.' What dribble! It's as if they do not know her at all. Look at this one, 'I cannot stop thinking about your hair in the dusk light-'. What rubbish."

Mothy continued to look at him, confused. "Hmm... Do you think these are empty because she...? Do you think she is the culprit?"

"You're asking if I think that she has since removed the bottles of alcohol and that is why the crates are so reduced?" Wolflock bit his lip. No. He didn't. But he didn't have the unequivocal proof. He couldn't just ask Yifi straight out. If she was the alcohol smuggler, he didn't want to alert her, but there were pieces here that felt like she wasn't. He played with his letter opener, then thumbed his new magnifying glass.

"That's it!" he exclaimed, slapping his hand across the crate as a grin spread across his face. "She's been giving away. It's all making sense. I see it now! Slavidus is a fool. Such a fool. You'll love this, Mothy, trust me. I will have you help me organise something to amend the whole situation, but you will indeed enjoy this."

"You've done that thing again where you had the

first part of this conversation in your head, but I trust you to know me. So, go ahead. What will I enjoy?" Mothy rolled his eyes and waved his finger in circles at Wolflock, gesturing for him to backtrack.

"Yifi is not our culprit." Wolflock clapped once to recentre his excitement into a comprehensive explanation. "She is hiding something though. All of these gifts are from her suitors that are still obsessed with her. There are two things to note. Yifi's mistreatment of their letters; they're crumpled, torn and shoved into a box with little care. The second thing to note is that many of the letters mention gifts they are no longer attached to."

"They also keep telling her how beautiful she looks. She hates that," Mothy added.

"Correct. Yifi, not wanting these gifts and boons, has been giving them away. Every single person has been given at least one gift from her since we reboarded the ship. Judging by the shape and size of the items I've seen; these boxes would easily be filled without being able to store alcohol bottles amongst them. But why, my friend, would she hide this?"

Mothy glanced around as if he was in a class and the teacher was waiting for an explanation.

"She has been wearing a new bracelet. One made of fishing line with lures adorning it. Who do we know who likes to fish?"

Mothy mimicked Wolflock, pinching his chin as he thought. Then he gasped and smiled from ear to ear. "Slavidus!"

"Slavidus." Wolflock nodded. "As per the box of letters she has collected and stored amongst her clothing, the items she appears to intend on keeping, we can deduce that she has collected Slavidus' love notes to her without his knowledge and kept them as treasures. She has refused all suitors gifts except for the one on her wrist. She didn't want Slavidus to know of the others for fear of upsetting him, especially when she thinks so poorly of them."

Mothy gasped. "She loves him!"

Wolflock's nod induced a delighted squeal from his friend.

"We have to tell him!" Mothy started to dart forward, but Wolflock grabbed his collar.

"Let's just wait and have a little peek at our other potential culprits, shall we?"

Mothy shrugged him off and took a breath to settle himself. "Alright, alright. I'm not sure I'll be able to contain myself though. Who else are we investigating?"

"Well, now that Slavidus and Yifi have been cleared from our suspects we are back to the following. Geagle, our prime lead. Although he has been an evident dullard, his information when he awakens will be invaluable. Then we have those who were clearly intoxicated during last night's dinner. Namely, Froderyk, Nan Ji and Haatji. Were any others suspicious after I departed?"

Mothy shook his head, but he looked displeased with Wolflock's list of suspects.

"I just don't feel like any of them would be so... well... dastardly."

Wolflock began pacing as he thought. "Indeed, but some things will drive a person to strange measures, my friend. For instance, Froderyk is a businessman. He is constantly looking for approval from those born into wealth and power. By obtaining vast amounts of wealth or even forms of nefarious power, he might finally feel worthy of his wife's position."

"But she loves him regardless!" Mothy protested.

"Irrelevant. These things come from how people feel, Mothy. They don't have to make sense; they just follow a pattern of human nature." He continued his pacing, speeding up as he pinched his chin. "Then we have Haatji. Seen consorting with Geagle during the day and also being intoxicated during the dinner. Although unlikely to be the orchestrator in all of this, I did find it strange that she had no symptoms of her previous evenings intoxication. She has been on the ship for how long?"

"She got on at Dua. No one really knows her though. She mostly stayed to herself. I won't lie, she is a bit hard to talk to. She only ever speaks in small sentences and avoids answering questions about herself. She gets a bit funny if men talk to her though."

"Funny, how?"

"Like... stiff. She won't let any male touch her either. Some Uluken women don't want men besides their husbands and family touching them, but they don't normally have an issue with young boys. Haatji does though. She wouldn't let the Nan brother's touch her when she was sick. Not like Parihaan though. She's the opposite. Really flirty. I think that's why Captain and Slavidus kept her away from Geagle. It was only after the Captain locked himself in his cabin for those two weeks did they even start speaking."

"We may have to devise an angle to obtain more data about both of them if we need to, but for now we can look through Froderyk and Nan Ji's cargo and see what that yields."

"Do we have to look through Nan Ji's things? I don't want to upset them anymore."

"You mean you don't want to upset Nü anymore."

Mothy didn't answer. He just shrugged.

"It wasn't your fault, you know? Surely she must

understand that."

He shrugged again.

Wolflock had been glad to have Mothy's full attention since the Krieger Zwerg dock, but he didn't like the awkward tension between Mothy and Nü.

"How about this: We look through Nan Ji's things to prove his innocence or we look for the twelve barrels that may lead us back to him anyway? I'll just collect the data, but we'll try to find what we need to help them be cleared of this mess."

Mothy's smile returned and he nodded. "I think I can do that. If we're quick."

"Brilliant! Let's get onto it then."

Wolflock squeezed all of Nan Ji's herb bags, feeling for any solid materials inside that were remotely bottle shaped. Nothing. Nan Ji had collected two crates worth of herbs at the Krieger Zwerg. They filled his storage space so much that some of his herb bags had toppled into his neighbours areas. Satisfied nothing was to be found in the bags, Wolflock opened one of the trunks. More herbs. The smell made his stomach feel queasy, but he persisted, driving his arm to the elbow into seeds, bark, twigs, leaves and dried berries. Nothing. Wolflock hopped down with a sigh, but his foot hit something hard and round, making him slip. His head smacked into the wooden box behind him and a sharp pain rang through his skull.

"You alright, Lockie?"

Wolflock gripped his hair, pressing hard onto his scalp. The pain was too strong to open his eyes right away. "Yeah... fine." he hissed. "Just..." He opened his eyes, the black spots in his vision fading. He trailed off as he caught sight of the bottle he'd slipped on. "Mothy... This is-"

"What are you doing to our herbs?"

Nü growled out from the stairs. She glared at them with her black almond eyes, as Wolflock raised the poorly made brown bottle, still with a trickle of bitter liquid inside.

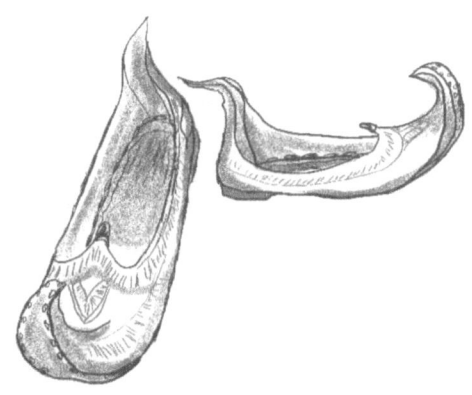

CHAPTER 5

Shoes and Booze

"Nü-mei!" Mothy pleaded as she charged forward, snatching the bottle from Wolflock, "It's not what you think. We just needed to make sure your father-"

"Mothy, shh!"

"Do not you dare speak about my father!" Nü hissed. There was a fire in her eyes and movements Wolflock found rather alarming.

"Nü-mei-"

Nü hissed like an angry cat, spitting several phrases Wolflock was sure were Xiayahn swears. He was rather impressed she could muster such vitriol.

"Nü, please."

"No! No please! You are not allowed in my family's space!"

Mothy recoiled, more hurt by the statement than he should have been.

"We have a problem, Nü. We need your assistance," Wolflock spoke as if she had addressed them as she normally would.

She turned to glare at him.

Keeping his tone nonchalant, he felt like a cat pretending to sleep as a mouse approached it. "Is that bottle your father's?"

"You found it in our space. Of course, it must be."

"Then we have a problem." he couldn't suppress his grin. He'd trapped her. The cat had his mouse and she'd lead him to the nest.

"What?"

"You see, we are currently hunting a smuggler and your father was behaving very peculiarly of late. He's been complaining about minor inconveniences as if he is very nervous. He has the means to order the smuggled goods on board and he would be able to make a great deal of money from it, no doubt. Now you confirm that the container in question was indeed his. This leads me to understand that he is the smuggler in question, and I shall have to take this to the captain. He commissioned me to investigate this for him."

Nü's face paled. "I... I..."

"Thank you so much for incriminating him so fully. It's made my job much easier, let me tell you. Here I was looking for evidence of guilt and Mothy was trying to find evidence of his innocence, but I guess I am the winner of this debate." He sighed with mock relief.

Nü's troubled eyes flicked from Wolflock to Mothy and back again. She trembled as she looked down at the bottle.

"Lockie!" Mothy finally snapped; albeit, Mothy's sharp tone was never particularly intimidating. "Don't treat our friend with such contempt. I'm sorry, Nü. Please forgive him." He stepped forward, blocking her from Wolflock's sight and cupping her arms. "He's only telling a partial truth. Your father isn't in trouble. We're just checking to see if we can find who brought those bottles onto the ship. I'm sorry."

Nü continued to shake, letting the bottle slip from her hand. Wolflock ducked forward and caught it, stepping away from the couple to examine it. It was identical. The same eye symbol with an X through it, the same sharp-edged rims. Wolflock poured the liquid onto his finger. It was tinged brown and stung his nose to sniff.

It tasted sharp with a mulled aftertaste.

"I did not know why father was so poorly behaved and without his wits yesterday. It disturbed me greatly. Mothy... I was frightened he would hit someone. He was so happy, then sad, then mad. It was as if his shen was disturbed."

"Nü, I needed to say something. I am so sorry for upsetting-"

Wolflock took a swig of the brown liquid for scientific purposes. It burned his entire throat, causing him to cough loudly and putting a stop to Mothy and Nü's conversation.

"You and Wolflock have never experienced fire water much before, have you?"

Both shook their heads.

"Nü, can you please show me your father's medical alcohol? The stuff he uses to clean his equipment." Mothy continued to speak softly, as if at any moment she'd start swearing at him again.

She nodded, grabbing a box of tinkling bottles from their storage. They were tiny little glass bottles, not more than a sip in each. The liquid was completely clear through the powdery glass.

"This is medicinal alcohol. It's used to clean wounds, equipment and some people gargle it for ulcers and throat infections, right?" Mothy nodded to Nü, who nodded back, her brows knitted with concentration.

"You don't swallow this stuff though. It's literally a poison. If you swallow this, you'll be sick." He passed it to Wolflock, who uncorked it and sniffed. It smelt like cold fire. Dipping his finger in to taste it, he felt it leave an acrid residue on his tongue that wouldn't disperse, no matter how much saliva he washed it with. It did seem to have a similar sharp bitterness to it as the brown liquid.

"Where I grew up, they would farm wheat, barley and potatoes to ferment and make this stuff. It would change colour sometimes. Sometimes red, sometimes brown, sometimes yellow," Mothy reminisced, rolling a small bottle between his fingers. "They would drink bottles of it. Everyone responded a bit differently. Some people vomited. Some people fought. They often got ulcers and different illnesses after their celebrations. Over the years their bellies would get big and hard like barrels, the whites of their eyes turned yellow and their noses went red. They got mad too. Real mad. You knew not to even look at them sometimes because they were looking for an excuse to fight. Some of my older friends would drink it and they'd sing, dance, fall over and cry, but it wasn't frequent, so they didn't get the long-term signs the others got."

"What about the people making it?"

"Kind of like a baker, they got sick of the taste of it. Some wouldn't drink it anymore because they'd drunk so much. Others would keep drinking it daily. Those ones got the shakes."

"Like the people who drank it last night?"

"Yeah, but they didn't just get it the night after. They got it when they hadn't had any."

"Ah!" Nü piped up; her eyes wide. "It is like a fire." The boys just waited and stared expectantly. "When you are normal, this drink gives you a fire. Like pouring oil onto it. Whoosh. You go up in a big flame. Then you find that you cannot sustain it the next morning and become little fire. This is why you shake. Your hot qi has cooled too fast and burnt up your substances. The big fire makes them shake, but the sharp cool makes them shake more when they are used to the big fire."

It made sense and didn't at the same time, so Wolflock let her continue.

"The people who use this as fuel have no... how to say it... It is like a fireplace but there is no log, just oil."

"I haven't heard it said like that before but sounds about right."

"So..." Wolflock pinched his chin, "because the makers drink it so frequently, they suffer more without it than when they have it. Mothy, are all alcohol production chains linked to... millers you're familiar with?"

Mothy nodded, appreciating Wolflock's discretion about his dark past. "Not small ones, but if we're looking for someone smuggling, maybe."

"Well that's definitive."

"Shh! Someone is coming."

Wolflock, Mothy and Nü heard the creaking footsteps above them. They froze for a moment, wondering if they'd go away, or if it was just a crew member grabbing a stashed snack. But they moved to the stairs.

"Quick! Hide!" Wolflock whispered, dashing under the stairs. Mothy and Nü jumped in between her father's crates, peeking over the top, obscured by the herb bags.

A pair of curly-toed, faded orange shoes creaked down the stairs. Wolflock saw the footsteps were quite uneven and the person leant on the railing for support. Besides that, all he could see was a person shrouded in a tattered old hooded cloak. They moved to the ship's main storage area, but they were far too slight to be crew.

They opened the barrels one by one, huffing and groaning as they didn't find what they were after. Wolflock, afraid they'd turn around and see him, began to squat down and slide behind the barrels. His heart beating in his chest like a hammer; he knew this was the culprit. They had to be. This had to be the person who had supplied the ship with drinking alcohol. He had to glimpse their face. That would solve everything.

Creeping slowly behind the barrels, he peered up. They wore the hood low over their face. Nothing. In the darkness of the hull he couldn't see anything. No hair, not even a chin.

The figure sighed with relief and plunged their arm into a barrel. It splashed and after a moment they drew out three brown bottles. Each dripped with water, but their craftsmanship was identical to the one Wolflock was still holding.

Damn, he thought sourly. He had been hoping the perpetrator would keep the alcohol stashed with their things and make his life easier. Now it was going to twice as hard to find out who was responsible for the smuggling. He could smell something, though. Not just the alcohol, but... pine?

He could hear them chewing. Were they chewing pine? They closed the barrel lid on their hand and hissed. Wolflock had to duck down so they didn't see him, but he heard them move about the room, opening other crates and barrels. How much did they think they could carry?

Heavier footsteps tromped upstairs and the four of them looked up. The hooded figure scurried away, Wolflock staring after them, his piercing blue eyes narrowed.

"Who was that?" Mothy whispered, helping Nü out of their hiding spot.

"That is the question. For now though, let's gather up the alcohol they stashed around the hull and take it to the captain."

The three of them dug out the hidden bottles from other people's luggage, gaps in between barrels and even tucked between sails.

"Hopefully that's all of them," Mothy said, readjusting the six bottles he held.

Wolflock held seven. Seven bottles of doubt.

CHAPTER 6
Thirsty Dreams Drunk Dry

Wolflock frowned. Something wasn't right. The three of them ascended the stairs into the crew quarters, then reached the stairs to the passenger cabins.

"Wait!"

Nü and Mothy turned to him.

"Take them to my room."

They looked warily at each other but shrugged and did as they were bid. Wolflock lead the way. As he came to the passenger hallway someone caught his eye. Captain Blutro was coming out of his room. The tall captain turned and stared, his eyebrows furrowed, and his mouth pressed into a disapproving line.

Wolflock shrugged, moving to his room. The captain had commissioned him to do a job and he was going to do it. There was no point worrying about the means when the ends would be discovered. He laid each bottle flat in his shoe draw, locking it with the room key.

"There. That will keep them safe. We can't give these to the captain yet. We don't have our smuggler. These can possibly be used as bait to get to them. Also, the captain has been a bit... unstable, shall we say, in regard to this. He might do something to alert the smuggler, which would drive them underground."

"I'm sure he's aware of this, Lockie," Mothy frowned, unconvinced.

"As am I. But emotions can make people act outside of their best interests. For now, let's continue our investigation. I would rather give him everything finished with a seal and tie, than with loose pages flying about."

"You mean you'd rather make sure you can show off to your full potential." Mothy added, inciting a chuckle from Nü.

"What's life without a bit of theatrics? What say you, Nü? Will you assist us?"

Nü smiled, shaking her head. "You will both be the end of me as Nan Nü."

Wolflock thought it was a strange saying, but he shrugged, understanding her answer to be a yes.

"What would you have me do?"

"Let me think first. Things have been odd on the ship of late and I must put them into place."

Mothy and Nü sat on his bed while Wolflock began pacing again. In his mind's eye he saw a great spiderweb weave before him. The strands leading towards the centre were clear. Slavidus' strand didn't reach the middle, neither did Yifi's, cut off by the clues that resolved and joined them.

Froderyk's and Nan Ji's threads may yet reach the conclusion. Haatji's thread remained thin, still drifting about in the breeze. The only thing linking her to any of this was her slur the previous evening and flirting with Geagle on the dock.

Each clue, each motivation, made the threads thicker and stronger, drawing them to the centre. Only the thread with the most definitive evidence would touch the centre, though.

With Nü sitting in his room, his thoughts focused around her father. He was able to order medicinal alcohol, so why not recreational? He had been in a foul mood since he'd nearly crashed into them at the post office. Had he been drinking even then? Mothy said alcohol affected ones temper too. Even this morning, the goblet he held up glittered because his hand shook. He had a history of foul moods' had he secretly been drinking all this time and received new stores at the Krieger Zwerg dock? He'd been complaining about everything more than usual, as well. Surely it wasn't just out of boredom.

It was beginning to make more sense and the Nan Ji thread grew thicker and brighter in Wolflock's mind.

"Nü. I need to see your father's account book."

Nü frowned, "You can see it, but I doubt you could read it."

"Will you translate for me?"

"I cannot."

"Cannot? Or will not."

"I will not tarnish my father's honour. Only bad children scrutinise their father's business."

"Oh?" Wolflock snorted, folding his arms. "So, changing your father's medicinal recipe isn't scrutinising your father's work? Don't be such a hypocrite, Nü."

Her face went cold. "I do not know what this word means, but I do not appreciate your tone."

"It's just to rule him off our list," Mothy soothed.

"Or to find him guilty faster."

Mothy gave him a wide-eyed stare, attempting to telepathically say, "Wolflock! Not helping!"

Wolflock stared blankly. He didn't care if Nü or anyone else on the ship thought he was rude. He wasn't trying to make friends with anyone anymore. They were simply a means to an end.

"I will not translate the specifics, but I will only do this if it will end your feud with him."

Wolflock shrugged, not caring if it did or didn't abide by Nü's wishes. Mothy was pleased at their truce though.

The three waited until lunch. Nan Ji didn't eat the dinners provided very often, or the breakfasts, but he did eat the lunches. Probably because they were simple sweet foods or fruit. They waited for him to ascend to the dining hall, and Nü took the boys to her family's cabin. It smelt like herbs and was lined with two bunk beds. Wolflock could see right away where each of them slept. Nü slept on the bottom right bunk, her comb, shoes and folded silk pyjamas with pink flowers stencilled onto them. Above her was Didi's bed where a few wooden toy soldiers lay by his pillow. Gege slept on the top left bunk, the foot of his bed stacked with educational scrolls, leaving Nan Ji's bed to be beneath his.

Nan Ji's bed was militantly straight, with what looked like journals and notebooks on his bedside table.

Within seconds Nü had his accounting booklet. It

was covered in red silk and embroidered with gold strands forming long snakelike dragons and phoenixes wrapped around golden letters only Nü could read. She flipped it open, humming as she read. Wolflock could see the different symbols in the far-right column that kept going down. It didn't take him long to see which numbers were one, two and three. The dates gave away the rest.

Then Nü's silence grew stony. She stared at the same two pages for too long. Wolflock looked at the numbers. Unlike all the other pages, this page had a strange arrow symbol next to the numbers.

"He... he could not be your smuggler." She spoke as if her chest were numb.

"I can see that. That symbol means negative, correct?"

She gripped the chest of her high collared shirt and closed her eyes as if it would all go away if she couldn't see it.

Nan Ji was a foul tempered man, but he had his children's best interests at heart. He didn't understand business out of Xiayah, though. His established clinic back home was very different to the other side of the continent, let alone travelling through different lands. Judging by the numbers on the dates, as well as by the dwindling symbols for finance, Wolflock knew he couldn't be their smuggler.

He wouldn't be able to have afforded the extra storage. The herbs he brought on board must have been arranged long before they reached the Krieger Zwerg.

As Wolflock stepped outside to let Mothy comfort Nü, he wondered if that was why the barrels went unsigned for? They were in terrible debt. That was plain to see. Nan Ji owed money. Had Nan Ji, in his desperation, made a deal he couldn't fulfil? Had it been him collecting and hiding bottles downstairs?

Glancing at the older man's shoes, he couldn't see any curly toed ones, and he had been wearing his plain grey ones as he ascended the stairs for lunch. No. It wasn't him. He wasn't that much of a fool. Of that, Wolflock could be certain. The thread in Wolflock's mind became clear, but it also had a clear stop. Only Froderyk and Haatji were left.

Thinking of Froderyk, Wolflock wondered if he had spoken with Geagle and convinced him to betray the ship? Had he paid him off? Froderyk was an apt businessman, so this theory was not farfetched. And his details had been right beside the aforementioned unsigned barrels.

How could he gather the information, though? He would have experience in being swindled. He knew the older man quite well, but something so nefarious would tear a rift in their fond acquaintance. What did he care though? He wasn't on the ship to make friends. He'd already lost them all by his Mabon comments. It didn't matter if he upset Froderyk. He may not be as forthcoming though... Wolflock lost sight of the hallway around him as he sank deeper in plot.

"Merry meet, Mr Felen," came a honeyed voice from his side. "Are you well? You look lost in thought."

Wolflock looked up to see Haatji. She was dressed in beautiful, glittering garments. A translucent veil covered most of her olive face, but her eyes shone through in their unique pastel green. She was as beautiful as Yifi but appeared unburdened by it. Even covered from head to toe in clothing, she radiated beauty and poise. Wolflock would not be swayed though. She was one of his lead suspects.

She must come from nobility in Uluken. If I want information I best be polite... for now.

"Merry meet, Miss Haatji. I am well. I just have a puzzle to solve. And you?"

"I am quite well. The ship is beautiful. I do love the water. I look forward to the cooler weather too. Miss Voof even gave me this today." She held out her arm, showing a beautiful gold serpent arm band wrapping its way around her clothed forearm.

Wolflock rolled his eyes. *Talking about the weather. What next? Fashion and gossip? How droll. Were all Uluken women as foolish and boring as this?*

"What is your puzzle?"

"It's somewhat of a riddle. One person has an item. You have to guess who has it, but you only get one attempt because if you ask the wrong person you lose the riddle."

He saw Haatji's cheeks rise in a smile as she thought. "I would say then to not ask anyone the question. Ask them the opposite of the question. Like the riddle where there are two dragons at a crossroad and one always tells the truth and one always lies. You must ask what the other would say to get the right directions." He couldn't help but notice that she kept her voice very low, but there was a distinct lisp to her 's's and 'th's.

Perhaps they aren't so boring. Wolflock pondered her words for a moment and felt his mind light up.

"You are right! That may be how we solve this riddle!"

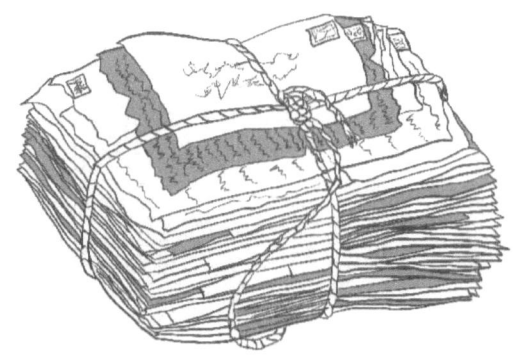

CHAPTER 7
Drowning in Morals

It didn't matter if everyone thought poorly of him. Wolflock didn't care, so pretending that he wanted to set up an illegal alcohol trade to the Mystentine University was an entirely viable way to get him his culprit. In his mind, it was glorious. If he didn't find the smuggler, then at least he would have lost nothing as everyone was going to stop talking to him after last night anyway.

In an instant he had it all planned.

He'd find some dirt on Froderyk by going through the papers he had hidden somewhere in his room. The same ones he'd picked up at the post office. Then he'd approach the businessman and see if he took the bait. If he didn't, he'd approach Geagle when he woke up with the same ploy. He'd also tell Geagle that he knew about Haatji, just to make sure he gave him all the information he needed.

He just had to wait for Fuhji and Froderyk to stop arguing.

Wolflock could hear them from his own room as long as his door was open, so he decided to pace to pass the time. He expected them to finish their heated discussion after a few minutes, but they just kept going. He'd occasionally hear them shout something about not listening or how they've changed. It was a circle. They just kept going over the same point, one not hearing the other.

How long could two people argue for? He huffed to himself. No. Too long. This just won't do.

He didn't care about disturbing the two people he'd made some of the most headway with, in regard to their friendship. He certainly didn't care that his gut was knotting as he rapped on their door.

"Excuse me," he announced. "I need to speak with Froderyk. I ask that you bookmark your argument and pick it up once I'm done."

Silence. *At least that's something.*

Froderyk opened the door, his brow creased with

more than just his normal short temper etchings. Fuhji knocked his arm out of the way as she pushed past him, escaping into the hallway and up to the deck. Wolflock's gut twisted harder when he saw there were tears sparkling on her cheek.

"Mr Felen?" Froderyk glanced around as if he were looking for an explanation or was being set up for a distasteful joke.

"Mr Timmerman. Mr Rags-to-Riches Timmerman. May I have a word?"

"Uh... yes? Granted you would have said to me that we'd had many a word by now."

"Ha. Yes. Yes, I would. I heard recently from a reliable source that you could help me with a business endeavour. Something Mystentine sorely needs while I'm studying there. Albeit, with the delays we've had I'm unlikely to make it in time for the Winter intake."

Froderyk's frown lightened as he became curious. He stepped aside and let the teenager into his cabin. The cabin had a different layout to Wolflock's. A plush double bed took up the majority of the room. To use the desk they had to use the edge of the bed as a seat. The desk was completely clean. Only a half-finished card game of cabale. No papers or writing materials were to be seen. Wolflock took special note of the wardrobe.

It's the only place he could hide something in here. Knowing Froderyk and his suspicious nature he'd have a safe. I'll have to crack the code.

"See," Wolflock paced back and forth, trying to keep his steps slow enough to hide his nerves, "I don't want to have to go all the way back to Plugh to my disappointed father only to have to return next year. I'd rather entertain myself with a new enterprise and make him proud by growing my independent wealth."

Lies, lies, lies. How do people do this all the time? It leaves a rancid taste in the back of my mouth.

"Ah. Well, that's something I can give you instruction on. What was it you were looking to sell? Service or product or both?"

"I was actually hoping you would be my supplier. See, I heard that Mystentine is very lacking in something that would liven the place up a bit."

"Oh? I've got a lot of contacts in Corl. What was your product? And don't say alchemical ingredients. You have to have proper training and registration to get those."

Wolflock grinned. "Oh no. I don't believe the government would supply registration to a man my age for this. I'm looking to import and distribute... booze."

Froderyk frowned, his face growing stony.

"Drinking alcohol. It makes for a good time and

could sell for a lot given its forbidden status."

"No."

"No?"

"I didn't think you were so simple minded to make a businessman repeat himself. No. Now be off with you. I will not entertain this absurd notion. You want to impress your father? How about not being a dishonourable scoundrel? How does that sound? Now get gone. I have work to do."

"But-"

"Out!"

Froderyk grabbed his shoulders roughly and drove the slender boy out of the room, slamming the door behind him.

"Really!" Wolflock huffed. "It was a simple question."

He hadn't gained much by his mock interview, but he did find out something. Froderyk was hiding something. Not just from the ship, but from Fuhji. His caginess about drinking alcohol was also strange. Wolflock had to find the letters he had seen Froderyk collect at the post office. He knew he had to search the room without Froderyk in there.

Wolflock scratched his black hair with his long fingers as he stalked back to his room and resumed his pacing. His only partial distraction was when Mothy re-entered.

"What are you plotting?" he joked with a half-hearted sigh.

"How are things with Nü?" Wolflock waved him off.

Mothy made a pin drop sign with his hand and fell back onto Wolflock's bed as he made crashing noises.

"That well then?"

"I just want to make it all better for her. I don't have any money though. If I could I'd just pay for all their travels and make their lives easier."

"You really like her, don't you?"

"Every time I look at her, I get fairies in my tummy. Every time she laughs, I see the sun. She's the cleverest, sweetest, funniest girl I've ever met."

Crashes... fairies... Nü...

"That's it! Mothy! Do you know how to make fireworks?"

"What?"

"Lights that explode in the sky? Normally used at festivals like Lammas?"

"Oh!" Mothy nodded slowly, not blinking. "No."

Wolflock pinched his chin and paced out of the room. He had a feeling someone else would know. He didn't even knock, he just pushed open the Nan family's door to see Nü cooling her porcelain face with a damp cloth.

"Nü. How do we make fireworks?"

She slammed her hands down and jolted upright. "What?"

Wolflock rolled his eyes. "Fireworks."

Nü took a moment to process his intrusion, tone and actual words.

"Do you mean yānhuā? Smoke flower?"

"I would have said fire streamers, but sure. Smoke flowers. Yānhuā." Wolflock began pacing up and down her room.

Nü cocked her head to the side. "You said it right."

"What? Yānhuā?"

"You said it right again. Your pronunciation is good."

Wolflock smirked. "I speak five languages, Nü. I intend on learning a few more in my travels. Do you know how to make yānhuā?"

"Yes, but I will not make it on the ship."

"I thought you'd say that. Fire hazard, yes?"

"It can catch places on fire, yes."

"What if I told you I wanted to make one that was fireproof? I just need to know how to make the original version."

Her eyes sparkled with excitement at the notion of

a chemical experiment. "Only use it on top deck, though. It is too dangerous under a wooden roof. I have seen it catch mansions on fire."

After a promise and a cough as they broke one of the hull fairy dust lanterns, Wolflock snuck some saltpetre, sugar, matches and butchers paper from the kitchen. They asked Matroos if they could use the kitchen for a stomach concoction Nü had made for Mothy, to which the dark-skinned man's eyes narrowed.

"What are you really doing?" he spoke with such a deep voice it made the air tremble. Like Hognut, his hair tried to eat his face. Instead of a beard, Matroos' hair was trying to eat him from the top down in the form of a spectacular afro.

"Exactly what I said we were doing."

Matroos' black eyes seemed to look under Wolflock's skin. After a moment he shrugged and threw a small iron pan to them.

"You clean it, or you work for me. *Qonda?*"

"*Qonda!*" Mothy jumped in before Wolflock could speak up.

Matroos turned away, finishing his preparations for lunch while the three got to work, cooking their sugar, saltpetre mix. Nü folded the butcher paper into candle shapes while the boys very carefully added the fairy dust to the cooling mix.

"Now, no one wants to see this from me. It will be received far better from both of you and with me out of sight. I'll help set you both up-" the pair glanced at each other with a subtle pink glowing in their cheeks as Mothy poured the mixture into the paper Nü held steady, "-and then give me a few moments to into my room. Make sure you make as much noise as possible. The aim is to see Froderyk. If you don't see him, we haven't finished. Make more and more noise. Stomp hard on his room. Wake him up and get him out."

They moved above Froderyk and Fuhji's room and Wolflock made sure the new spectacle would be able to disturb him as much as possible. Wolflock looked up for a final check only to see a great reddish beard with an unlit pipe poking out through the bushy hairs.

"What in Houl's name are yeh lot doin'?" Hognut grunted, striking a match on his tattered matchbox.

"Making fireproof fireworks out of fairy dust so Wolflock can check Froderyk's letters for the Captain." Mothy grinned as if that was the most reasonable response ever.

Wolflock shrugged with nonchalant smile as the grouchy crewman shook his head.

"O' course yah are..." Hognut sighed, lit his pipe

and walked away.

Snickering, the three of them finished lining their display and secured it so it poured over the side of the ship.

"Perfect. Now, make a show and dance for as long as you can. By my calculations it should last for long enough. Just keep Froderyk up here." Wolflock began walking to the stairs.

"And you are sure this is not going to create heat?" Nü asked as her smile was replaced with a serious expression. Wolflock could hear Mothy begin striking a match, but it must have flicked too close to the fairy smoke flower. In his alarm he pinched the match and hissed as he shook his burnt fingers.

Wolflock smirked, glancing half over his shoulder back at them.

"More or less."

Ignoring her incoming objections, Wolflock dashed down the stairs and slipped into his room, diagonally across from Froderyk's and Fuhji's room. The suspenseful quiet that followed seemed to last for an age. He had the urge to begin pacing again, but he didn't want to miss the moment Froderyk left. He began flipping the little pencil sized flare he'd made between the fingers of his left hand. He felt jittery. He knew he'd have to get the information and get out as quickly as he could, so he attributed his nerves to that, but he couldn't help but feel like he was doing the wrong thing.

This will pass, Wolflock. Fickle friendships of people you'll never see again isn't worth the anxiety of Mabon. Remember that. Are you really going to be sending them letters and silly little gifts every year? No. It's not worth the bother. What could they possibly offer in return for that friendship? They aren't intellectual. They aren't going to study. Nothing. They can offer me nothing.

Heart set in stone, he listened to the cheers on the deck and, as Bleen and Faleen came out of the room directly across from his, he saw the showers of glittering gold and blue sparkles pouring over the side of the ship. The stomping, chanting and dancing began to grow in volume. Still no Froderyk.

Did he have his window closed? Was he sleeping?

Wolflock grabbed the box of matches in his desk drawer and slipped to Froderyk's closed door as the rest of the ship's company raced to see what the commotion was. When the coast was clear, he struck a match and lit the end of the tiny fairy smoke flower. After a second it began to shoot and pour out with blue and gold sparkles. Grinning, he dropped it and kicked it under the door, stepping into Bleen and Faleen's bohemian styled room.

"What the blazes?!"

Wolflock snickered as he heard Froderyk stomping, swearing and finally storming out of the room. He was shouting about how whoever disturbed him would pay for it, to which Nan Ji shouted that he would not have it added to his bill.

Still grinning, Wolflock slipped into the room and threw open the wardrobe doors. A safe sat under the half-folded clothing hanging from the wooden coat hangers. Just as expected. Iron, sturdy, and locked with a combination lock. The safe was old though. There were clear markings from the oil on Froderyk's fingers and traces of scratches. It was a simple run of the mill iron safe. Likely to be six digits, often of significance to the person, such as a date.

He pressed his ear to the cold metal and began turning the dial. He could hear a thick pin drop whenever he hit the right number in the right direction.

Two... eight... zero... nine... Now what? Twenty eighth of Xissyli Sor... but what year?

"Mr Felen?"

Wolflock swallowed, ear still pressed to the safe, as Fuhji moved the cupboard door to see him fully. He was caught. He'd be given hard labour or might even have worse disciplinary action for this. This looked actively stealing. The Captain might let him off, but then he'd be even less liked on board. What did that even matter though? He didn't care. No one liked him after his display at Mabon anyway.

"Twenty eighth of the ninth, in the second year of King Rayin's rule."

Wolflock entered the last two digits and the safe clunked open. "Fuhji... why?"

"I... I need to know. My husband has become something frightening lately. He is snappy, secretive and afraid. He won't tell me what trouble he's in. He never hides anything important from me. I'm frightened he's..."

"Do you think he's the one selling alcohol?" Wolflock didn't pull the stack of bound letters out right away. He felt his heart ache for Fuhji's worries. He would hate for Myna to ever get into nefarious activities through her political pursuits. He could understand Fuhji's concerns.

"I don't even want to hazard that guess. Please. Help me."

With a nod, he hauled the letters out and they both began sifting through them.

"Why hadn't you gone through these before if you knew the code?"

"I respect and love my husband. He is a good man, but it wasn't until today that I felt that there was something deeply wrong. We always promised to never sleep on an argument and last night we did. It continued this morning. I refuse to live like this or let him live alone with this anxiety."

"Has he trafficked drinking alcohol before?"

"No. But when he was intoxicated on Mabon, I was very worried he was in dire need of help. I was worried that he was going broke and didn't want to tell me, but I don't care. I would be with him even if we lived in a dirt shack digging potatoes. He knows many... less honourable people in business, but he has always actively chosen to refuse trade with them."

Wolflock half listened as he read through the letters.

Two thirds were pleas and cries from his previous employees, managers and the families of both. They were begging him to return. The competition was too strong without his innovation, they were going under. They were stagnating and dying.

The other third were from insurance companies advising that his businesses should be sold, in which he would receive exorbitant amounts of money. But the staff would be dissolved and rearranged, not guaranteeing their future employment. Wolflock sat back with a sigh, staring at the painted wall.

"He's not broke. His businesses are going under

without his attention. His staff are begging him to come back as he is sailing away."

"He sees his businesses as his first children! I'm going to be sick!" Fuhji's eyes welled with tears and she leaned forward, sobbing into the letter she held, resting her head on Wolflock's knee. "We can't go back. He'll be killed! What are we going to do?"

Wolflock was taken aback by her sudden outburst, but he patted her dark brown hair, hoping it was of some comfort. He could see in the little waste bin by their bed a glistening brown bottle. There was only a little bit of liquid in the bottom, but the rim was still wet.

Fuhji's loud crying seemed to drown out the noise of whatever Mothy and Nü were continuing to do upstairs, as well as any noises of people coming down the stairs. This became even more apparent when Froderyk, red faced, banged open the door, looking wildly around the room. His letters were scattered everywhere, the cupboard and safe were open, and Fuhji, his beloved bride, was sobbing into another man's (albeit much younger man's) lap.

"What," he snarled through gritted teeth, "have you done to my wife!?"

"I-"

Froderyk leaped forward, seizing Wolflock by the

shirt and lifting his wiry frame of the bed. Fuhji gasped and scrambled around, trying to separate them.

"Frodey! Stop!"

"What did you do to my wife!?" Froderyk roared, spittle flying over Wolflock and the stench of acrid breath drenching him.

"I did nothing! Unhand me man! You're clearly not of your senses!" Wolflock tried to push his hands away but his thin hands against the burly tradesman hands made no match.

"You rude little cretin! I'll show you what happens to boys like you on the docks in Corl!"

"What's this ruckus?" Slavidus boomed, hearing the disruption from the hallway.

"Frodey! Stop-blergh!"

Froderyk did drop Wolflock, but it was only because Fuhji began projectile vomiting breakfast over the edge of their bed. Wolflock looked between them and had to leap back as Froderyk turned green and copied his wife. Both emptied their stomachs onto the floor, Wolflock caught between them. He grabbed the waste bin and an empty washbowl, passing it to both of them as he awkwardly patted their backs. Slavidus raced off to get damp towels and a mop. Finally finished, wiped and the floor washed (Wolflock outright refused to do such a menial task, so Froderyk was forced to acquiesce as punishment for causing the disturbance), Fuhji felt faint and was laid down on fresh sheets. As Wolflock tidied the papers around them, Froderyk stroked his wife's hair as she fell asleep.

"What in the Houl's name was that all about, Froderyk?" Slavidus scratched his head, pulling a few strands of salt and pepper hair free from his ponytail.

Froderyk couldn't look up. "I'm sorry, First Mate Oncor. I... was not myself."

"You're worried about your businesses. Aren't you?" Wolflock frowned and crossed his arms, feeling salty that he had been assaulted.

"You're right on target, Mr Felen. I am. It's no excuse to behave as such."

"It's more than that though. You came from nothing and you built everything you have. It's hard to leave and it's even harder for you to know your businesses are suffering. They're lacking your innovation and they think they need you there. Plus, now that you've received insurance offers, they'll think you're just going to dissolve their livelihoods."

Froderyk sniffed and put a fist to his eye, hiding his tears.

"And you're torn because-"

"Because you love her, but you love your work," Slavidus interjected, making them both look up, alarmed that he'd spoken.

"Aye... Aye you're both right. I don't know what to do. All I need is an edge. A new supplier I can send things down to them that none of the competition will have."

"And you have a product in mind?" Wolflock nudged. Froderyk was drunk, so he may just be drunk enough to reveal secrets about the alcohol trade.

"Nothing... I've got nothing. Nothing my competition can't already get access too. Nothing I can have sole rights to import. They won't last the next half a year if I don't find something."

"Why didn't you just tell Fuhji? She has been distraught over all this. She helped me break into your safe because she wanted to help you!" Wolflock exclaimed.

Froderyk looked up at them both, washing his face again with the cool towel. "She deserves better. Better than the life I can offer her. She is so precious and all I can do is keep trying to give her the life she deserves. I knew I was doing the wrong thing by hiding things from her. My pride was wounded, and I was ashamed that I left my affairs back in Corl in the state where they could degrade so rapidly. If I could give them all a magic potion to make them more creative or courageous I would... but unfortunately innovation is rarer than I thought it was."

Something about the words "magic potion" echoed through Wolflock's mind.

"I may very well be able to fix this... but you must swear an oath," the young man glared at the tradesman, who nodded cautiously. "When Fuhji wakes up you have to be honest with her. She needs you to communicate with her. Tell her everything. She doesn't need the stress of worrying about you too."

Froderyk chuckled and sighed, resting his hand on Fuhji's side. Wolflock left the room, but not before seeing a torn look across Slavidus' tanned face. Even though he told himself that he didn't care, Wolflock couldn't help but feel a sense of gratification that Slavidus might make moral progress without knowing Yifi was cleared of all charges.

After a few minutes, some hasty explaining, and being told a sentus wouldn't be paid for the information, Wolflock brought the hesitant Nan Ji to Froderyk's room. He was grateful that the tradesman had sobered up a bit more by the time he returned.

"Froderyk, Nan Ji has an abundance of herbal potions and ingredients that may be just the thing to give your people their needed magic potion."

Froderyk blinked, then caught himself and stood up

to shake Nan Ji's hand. "Merry meet, my man. Is this true? Do you have exotic herbs and remedies not available in Corl?"

"Uh..." Nan Ji processed the mumbled accent, squinting as he did so. "Yes. I have herbs only found in Xiayah. Many of which I have grown in the best farms in the country. I also have remedies that are only known to my family. Passed down from father to son."

"This is wonderful! We need to go over the details, but if that's the case I'll need to buy large amounts from you to have shipped back to Corl at the very next dock. Can you do that for me? If we settle on a contract I can pay today and then organise regular shipments before Yule."

Nan Ji jerked back as Froderyk spoke too quickly for him to understand. "I... I... yes! Yes! Let us look at this deal. This will be very good. I was going to sell my remedies in Creast, but this is much better."

"Thank you, Wolflock," Froderyk pulled the skinny teenager into a bear hug. Wolflock could have sworn he heard a rib pop. "Thank you for this introduction. This may just save my people back in Corl."

Wolflock extricated himself from Froderyk's firm embrace, straightening his clothes. "It's not a worry, my good man. If anyone understands the need to maintain one's pride, it would be me."

As gratifying as it was to see the tension ease for two of his fellow passengers, Wolflock felt an uneasy crawling sensation on his back. This ruled out Nan Ji and Froderyk as suspects. As well as Yifi and Slavidus being discarded earlier. It was now either Geagle or Haatji, both of which seemed unlikely to be the true culprits. He contemplated that after ruling out all other options, the most unlikely one would have to be the true course.

He huffed, going to the dining hall for a late afternoon tea, trying to see the plausibility of Haatji or Geagle being the smuggler. Geagle let the barrels be brought onboard and go unsigned for. He was intoxicated during Mabon. He had soft spots for women that gave him any attention. Those thoughts intertwined the thread of reasoning in Wolflock's mind to Haatji. Haatji had been seen flirting with Geagle on the docks that morning. She also wore peculiar shoes like the pair that he'd seen coming down the stairs to the hull earlier. But what motive could she have? Geagle may have been pandering to her, but why did she want to smuggle alcohol on board?

"Lockie!"

Wolflock hadn't realised he had walked around the deck as he thought. He was struck by the realisation that he was right at the stern of the ship as Mothy ran up to him.

Rhiannon D. Elton

"Lockie! It's Geagle! He's awake!"

CHAPTER 8

Over the Barrel

W here is he now?"

"He's being treated by Nan Ji's son, Gege. They're still in the crew quarters."

Wolflock charged off. Finally, it would all be narrowed down. Geagle would be easy to get answers from. He vaulted the stairs to the guest rooms and crashed into Captain Blutro. Wolflock went sprawling across the hall, but the captain caught himself on the wall.

"What in Houl's name are you doing, Mr Felen!?"

"Solving the mystery, Captain. Watch yourself next time." Wolflock picked himself up and carried on, ignoring the perturbed look Captain Blutro sent after him.

He slid down the bannister to the crew cabins and grinned wickedly. Geagle was pulling a face as he gulped down a cup of whatever Gege had given him. The crewman looked awful. His watery blue eyes were bloodshot, and he sported huge bags under his eyes. He held his stomach like he was going to be sick.

"Good work, Gege," Wolflock interrupted. "I'd like a private word with Geagle if you don't mind." Gege nodded, disappearing up the stairs without a word, as Wolflock turned to the unsuspecting crewman. "Now, we're going to have a little chat, Geagle. See, I know. I know it all. I just need you to fill in the gaps."

Geagle looked more and more confused by the second.

"I know about the drinking alcohol. I know about how you let it get brought on board and didn't ask for a signature."

Geagle paled. "N-no, Mr Felen. It's not like that. I wouldn't!"

"I know that the Captain has forbid any drinking alcohol on board. Now, that is something I want to know about first. Why?"

"Why what?" the tall Corshman swallowed.

"Why doesn't the Captain like drinking alcohol?

Why to the point where he would ban it completely from his vessel?"

"I-I dunno. I just know it ain't allowed."

"And yet you brought it on board regardless?"

"N-no sir. I didn't know. I swear I didn't know. She-they-it wasn't meant to be anything like that."

Wolflock sneered. He had him on the ropes. Poor dullard didn't stand a chance. Plus, Wolflock hadn't even drawn his ace yet.

"So, let's get this straight. A 'she' or a 'they' convinced you to let twelve barrels come onto the ship without knowing the contents and without signing for them? When there is explicit instruction from the Captain, due to legal purposes, to register all goods?"

"I-I-I-"

"And furthermore, it happened while you were left in charge of these precious documents? My dear man, you see how this looks bad for you, right?"

"I swear it weren't me, Mr Felen. I didn't mean to upset no one. I didn't mean for the Captain-"

"To find out? Nevertheless, he did. Now, you have a few options. You can tell me who orchestrated this operation and I shall endeavour to tell the Captain that you had no true part in this due to your naivety and ignorance, or-" he paused for dramatic effect, smirking as beads of sweat appeared under Geagle's wispy blonde hair, "-I will have to tell the Captain it was all your doing and that he has put his trust in the wrong man, as did Slavidus."

Geagle quivered and spoke as carefully as he could, but his shoulders squared.

"I... You'll need to tell the Captain it was all me then. I got distracted and just waved the barrels on before I realised anyone had signed for 'em."

Wolflock jerked back. He hadn't expected that.

"What?"

"It was all m'fault. I didn't know what was in 'em, but they was in our shipping bay, so I sent 'em on."

"And how did someone find out that there was drinking alcohol in them then?"

Geagle swallowed. Immediately he knew he couldn't keep up a lie like this. "That's it. I dunno. I got nothing. But it were all me fault."

Wolflock glared at him. "You're a terrible liar. You know that I know who has brought these barrels on board. I know full well who it is. I just wanted definitive proof from you."

"Do ya have any proof?"

Wolflock quickly tossed up whether or not to bluff. He only had the glimpse of curl toed shoes. If he gave that information to Geagle, he might tell Haatji to hide her shoes or destroy the evidence. If he told Geagle he had nothing, which was closer to the truth, the burly man might get a wind of confidence and dig his heels in on the matter.

"I have evidence. I'm not at liberty to share it until my investigation is over though." He wanted to kick himself as the words escaped his mouth.

He'd given away the game. Geagle knew what he was looking for and now any other evidence would be hidden too. This was what the Captain meant by not giving away what he was searching for until he actually had it.

"We have everything we need. I was just hoping to clear your name of the matter. The crew mean a lot to the Captain. He'd be disappointed in such behaviour."

Geagle bit his lip and looked away. "I don't want to upset the captain, but I can't. I can't hurt her like that."

"Listen, Geagle," Wolflock sighed and rolled his eyes, "I know Haatji distracted you while you were on the docks. I also remember you had found a new love and were telling your previous lovers that you had to leave them. Remember? I wrote those letters six times. It's plain to see you two are very fond of one another. If you help me understand the situation then I'll be able to make sure you both get into minimal trouble."

Geagle's watery eyes shot up as Wolflock mentioned Haatji. But they weren't filled with worry. More like...

relief.

Wolflock's gut twisted. His mental web unravelled a little. Did he have the wrong thread in place?

"The alcohol will have to be removed though. Probably disposed of. It's important we get all of it."

Geagle swallowed again, this time his eyes darted around the crew quarters as if he wanted to escape. His rapid mood change, and body language, told Wolflock some unsettling things. Was Geagle addicted to drinking alcohol? Had he promised someone something in regard to it?

He didn't have time to think about it any longer before he heard heavy, angry stomps coming down the stairs.

"Enough," Captain Blutro growled. "Geagle. Get up on deck. I don't want you to be anywhere below deck until we get to Creast. I heard everything. Never have I felt so betrayed by one of my own. You're on half rations for a month. Now get out of my sight."

Geagle went whiter than a ghost, bending his head down as he scurried past Captain Blutro. Wolflock turned and frowned at the Captain.

"I'm not finished yet. I haven't gotten definitive evidence-"

"Oh no, lad. You're finished." Captain seethed,

breathing furiously through his flared nostrils. "You're done. No more investigating and no more privileges."

"What?"

"I trusted you to locate the booze and find who was smuggling it."

"And I have been doing both, so what's the problem."

"This."

Captain Blutro threw down the bag he was carrying. Clinking brown bottles spilled forth from the sack. Wolflock stared.

"I saw you and your friends smuggling these into your room. You were as subtle as a brick about it. Did you think I'd let it slide? Did you think you could have it as early payment for a half-baked job? Were you planning on having a good old raucous time with your pals, eh?"

"What? No! I-"

"The mystery is solved, lad. I'll send the crew down to search the hull and rooms for these bottles in barrels. Knowing they're in the ship's storage and not the passengers is all I need. Then we'll burn them off. Geagle was misled by Haatji and the others stumbled upon it by accident. Clearly these barrels weren't meant to be shipped by us. It was a logistics mistake. That's it. Now get out of my sight. I'll hear no more on the matter."

"But-"

"Not another word from you, Mr Felen."

"I-"

"I said 'not another word'!"

"You can't just ignore the lack of evidence!"

"I said not another word. Now if you persist, I'm going to put you on kitchen cleaning duty, understand?"

"That's not fair!"

"Ah! So, you'll be helping this evening at dinner, as well as breakfast and lunch tomorrow."

"You can't do that!"

"Add another four more shifts to your load."

"This is outrageous!"

"You must really enjoy cleaning," the Captain hissed.

Wolflock shut his mouth and glared seethingly. The Captain glared back with equal ferocity. Silence. Burning silence.

"Good. Ten cleaning shifts will drill some discipline into you. Now, my final word on the matter is that it has been dealt with. If I hear you start this up again, I'll put you under cabin arrest. Understood?"

Without a word, Wolflock barged passed the Captain, fuming. He stomped to his room and slammed his door closed so hard that the fairy dust lantern rattled in the hall. Wolflock threw himself down on the bed, thrashing his pillow.

How could the Captain think so poorly of him? He wasn't some lying vagabond! He had always acted in the best interests of the Captain when he'd asked him to do a job. Why didn't he trust him enough to do the work this time? Why was he being so infuriating? What made him so irrational and out of character?

After properly exhausting his arms, Wolflock's rage had been quelled to a light simmer.

He took deep, deliberate, slow breathes. It helped him to think.

What if... He began throwing thoughts around to re-establish his mental web of the case, *... there was something else to do with the captain and alcohol? He seemed put off even by Nan Ji's medical alcohol, but drinking alcohol made him far more irrational. Captain Blutro had invaded his room in the middle of the night. He'd made poor assumptions about Wolflock's character and baseless assumptions about his crew and company. He was content to let the entire situation go unresolved in its entirety and for what?*

He had to make sense of it. Perhaps it would tell him more about why the alcohol had been smuggled on board in the first place. He also had to investigate Haatji. But his gut bent away from the thought of her. Her name had not evoked the same response in Geagle as Wolflock had hoped. Geagle was clearly trying to get himself in trouble so his lover wouldn't be in any blame, but Wolflock wasn't quite sure it was Haatji.

Shaking his head, he sat up and went to Mothy's room.

Nothing.

He must still be upstairs, he thought to himself. I'll find him and we'll make a plan to collect more data.

He had no intention of dropping this before it was resolved.

As Wolflock made his way to the stairs he had to stand aside as five crew were pulled from their deck duties and the night shift staff were woken up to search the hull. Geagle was swabbing the deck with his shoulders slumped and his expression despondent.

It only took a moment to find Mothy and Nü having afternoon tea on one of the picnic blankets with her brothers, as well as Tinni and Tanni.

"Merry meet, Lockie," he smiled brightly, but it faded as he saw Wolflock's dark expression. "Are you ok?"

"Aye. I'm fine. I..." He needed to speak to Mothy alone. "How did the smoke flowers go?"

"They didn't set fire to anything," Nü said a bit stiffly as she sipped her tea.

"They were stunning. Really special. The company loved them. It was like magic."

"Well," Wolflock shrugged, "fairy dust is technically magical. Mothy, can I-"

Before Wolflock could finish, Slavidus stood by the wheel and rang the ship's silver bell, sending noise through the entire vessel. One by one the company gathered in front of him. Rows of barrels had been collected, clustered on the deck. The crew stood stoically behind them.

The kitchen cauldron sat amongst the barrels. Wolflock watched as the crew, stone faced, didn't make eye contact with anyone. It was as if they were soldiers. The only one who wasn't present was Geagle, who was swabbing beside the dining hall behind the ensemble as Stra spoke to him.

"I would like to say, 'merry meet'," Captain Blutro boomed over the deck, standing in the same stiff manner as the crew. " But this is not a merry day. We have come to discover a few things and I would like to address them before we sail any further into the Dragon's Spine. Firstly, Mr Wolflock Felen. Please come front and centre."

Wolflock frowned. He wasn't afraid. The Captain already had punished him, so he didn't care what came next. He did see a chance to view the crowd though. Perhaps seeing their responses would give away the true culprit.

He stepped around the barrels. They were all different ages, colours, and were adorned with different company stamps.

All different companies. Whoever brought on the original twelve barrels either hid the alcohol amongst new barrels, or they deliberately ordered different cases to avoid suspicion. They had been so clever. How did it all go wrong?

"As you all should be aware, drinking alcohol is prohibited on the Silver Ice Hair for safety reasons, as well as moral ones."

Wolflock recalled the Captain saying that those who drank alcohol couldn't perform their duties, got sick and fought, but moral reasons?

"Alcohol is an evil liquid and it should only be used for medical purposes. Even in the case of medicine it shouldn't touch a body," Captain Blutro continued. His voice was steady, but Wolflock saw his hands shaking in anger. "Those who drink it for pleasure are corrupted, idiotic, debased beings and have no right to be on my ship. If I catch anyone consuming alcohol, I will lock them in their cabins with half rations. And if I find someone has been smuggling it, this is what will happen."

He raised his hand as a thick cloud covered the sun,

casting a dark shadow over them. The crew collected the bottles of drinking alcohol and began pouring them into the cauldron.

Wolflock looked around the company.

Yifi, Nan Ji and Froderyk all looked ashamed. They cast their eyes down, and they refused to watch the scene directly. Most others looked on in confusion. Parihaan's eyes brimmed with tears, but Wolflock attributed that to the rousing the Captain had just given.

Haatji looked stoic. Too stoic. As if she knew she was being watched and needed to protect herself. She raised her pastel green eyes and looked directly at him.

Wolflock glanced away to avoid her suspicion. Had he been wrong? That stare.. His gut knotted as he considered that he didn't have all the information he needed on her. She was hiding something. The crew finished emptying what would have been nine barrels worth of drinking alcohol.

"This evil plague upon my ship will be no more." Blutro clicked his fingers and Hognut lit the cauldron on fire with a match.

Wolflock watched for the responses. A few people clapped awkwardly. The children just liked seeing something lit on fire. But it was the gasp through the flames that Wolflock homed in on. Parihaan had clapped her hands to her mouth, shaking as she stared past him. The gasp caused him to lose sight of the other Uluken woman, who was suddenly nowhere to be seen.

CHAPTER 9

A Drunk Man's Words

It just wasn't right.

Something was missing. The threads didn't touch the centre. There were so many details that hadn't been accounted for and so many that didn't fit. It was a puzzle that needed solving, and Wolflock would be damn sure to solve it.

As the crowd dispersed, he waited for Mothy to come over to him.

"Everything alright? You looked like you'd been told you'd get coal for Yule. What's happened?"

Wolflock glared around the deck, making sure no

one was listening. Geagle and Stra were still in conversation to his left, but at least it wasn't the captain or his prime suspect.

"Listen. The Captain rushed me. He saw us putting the bottles in my room and thought we were being childish."

"Huh?"

"He thought we were going to drink them. Fool. Like I would drink anything of such terrible quality."

Mothy chuckled.

"So, he's going to be watching me like a hawk. He has the crew on guard too. Minus Geagle, who's being punished for his involvement. I want to know why he's being so irrational about all this."

"Ah. So, I assume you won't just go up and ask him, no?"

"I'm not in as much favour as you normally are. I... uh... don't think that would work for me, no."

"Then what's your next goal?"

"I want to read through some of his old logs and see if I can find incidents where he's had to make decisions about drinking alcohol."

"Hmmm... That means you'll be sneaking into his quarters."

"Aye."

"Which means you'll need a distraction or some way to go through his journals."

"Aye."

"Well... I'm all out of ideas. What do you think?"

It was Wolflock's turn to laugh. "No more fairy dust smoke flowers? No spontaneous party on deck?"

"Honestly, Lockie, the captain said drop it. We got the drinking alcohol, and no one got too upset. Geagle was bound to get in trouble for letting someone bring things on board that weren't signed for. But besides that, I don't think we should try to get into more trouble."

"Alright, where is Mothy and what have you done with him?"

Mothy rolled his eyes, leaning next to the dark-haired boy on the taffrail. "You've been acting strangely since the Captain said we'd have a Mabon celebration. You're normally far more subtle in your plans. What's with all the razz and dazzle lately?"

"I'm just getting more comfortable-"

"At what? Upsetting people?"

"If you don't like the way I do things I can do it myself!" Wolflock snapped and tried to step off, but Mothy caught his arm and brought him back to the railing.

"I didn't mean it like that. I meant: Why are you upset? You're acting more... impulsively than you normally do. Like you want to mess up."

Wolflock's lips flattened. Mothy had him pinned to the grey polished wooden railing as much as he did in the conversation. His friend was right though. He had made blunders in an attempt to draw out the case. He could have solved it much faster, but that would mean having to socialise with everyone and listen to their judgements after his Mabon speech. He didn't want to let them get to him and make him feel rejected. He didn't want to give anyone the chance to make him feel like a child again.

"If you help me solve this case, and apparently, keep my head in check, I'll tell you everything."

Mothy elbowed his arm affectionately and nodded. "Of course, I was going to help you, anyway. I can't resist these mysteries on board any more than you can. What have you discovered since we last spoke and where are we looking now?"

Relieved, Wolflock explained. "We've crossed off Slavidus, Yifi, Froderyk and Nan Ji. Geagle was an accomplice. Whether or not he knew what he was being an accomplice to before the barrels came onto the ship remains to be seen. That leaves us with," he lowered his voice, "Haatji."

"She is very mysterious," Mothy nodded, squinting a little as he thought. "What makes you think it's her?"

"To begin with, I saw her flirting with Geagle on the dock. She was slurring at dinner, she's very secretive about her personal information, she's wealthy, which means she might have been selling alcohol on black markets for a long time now. I can only assume its lucrative. Then there is also her dress. When we saw that person come down the stairs and pulled out all those bottles earlier, they were wearing orange shoes with a curled toe. No one else here wears shoes like that except people from Uluken."

"That makes a lot of sense. I mean... I like Haatji. She's nice. Strange, but nice. I kind of feel like she has a lot of secrets though. I didn't want anyone to be your culprit, but I guess it makes sense."

"That it does. We have to get data on where she may be hiding the alcohol. The rooms and hull have been searched, but judging by the amount burnt, there should still be at least two barrels remaining."

"How do you figure that?"

"Elementary, my dear Mothy. Gauging the size of the bottles and how they can be placed within a barrel, each barrel could fit eighty bottles inside it. Twelve unsigned for barrels came aboard during Mabon." Wolflock began pacing back and forth, using his fingers as a visual display to show his calculations to Mothy. "Hence, we can safely assume that nine hundred and sixty bottles existed on the ship."

"Twelve lots of eighty. Got it." Mothy repeated with a short nod.

"Approximately, each suspect drank one bottle and I suspect two more have been consumed today, making eight bottles being consumed."

"Nine hundred and sixty minus eight. Aye."

"We saw twenty bottles being moved in the hull and took them to my room." Wolflock continued, glad Mothy was keeping up."

"Nine hundred and fifty two minus twenty, then?"

Wolflock nodded. "Those bottles and the bottles the crew found in the remaining nine barrels, were burnt away."

"So... nine lots of eighty... is..."

"Seven hundred and twenty." Wolflock added impatiently. "If we believe that the bottles that were removed from the barrels can be counted within that seven hundred and twenty, that leaves two barrels. One hundred and sixty bottles left. More than enough to cause trouble for the ship, especially as we embark through the treacherous Dragon Spine Mountain Range."

"Uh..." Mothy paused, counting numbers on his hands before shrugging. "What's wrong with travelling through the mountain range?"

"Well, it's an aside, but living in Plugh you learn a lot of history about Grothener and its neighbours." Wolflock shrugged, sitting down at his desk and turning the chair so he could sit side on to Mothy. "The Dragon's Spine is the range of mountains on the northern border of Grothener, Uluken and Syongdelen. It only has two passes that allow access to Shiriling above it. For hundreds of years people could only get through via the Uluken trails, but they'd have to cross the desert to reach it."

"That's where Hazzim was from. Uluken. I hope to meet him there one day." Mothy perked up at the mention of somewhere he knew. His eyes had dulled with all the barrel mathematics.

"If you know what city he's in we might go together. Anyway, it was important during the war against the evil King of Chaysaile to find a place where his armies couldn't reach the refugees. Initially, the town of Ravenswood was founded for just that, but the King sent a secret army to destroy them. The survivors passed through the Dragon's Spine and made their way to Shiriling. Once they made it through, they established Mystentine, as well as trade routes. With the help of the natives, they were able to navigate the waters of the Zilber River back down into Grothener and Syongdelen for secret trade."

Mothy nodded eagerly, but Wolflock only realised

at the end of his speech that his eyes had glazed over.

"Nod twice if you're really a maramuti in disguise?"

Mothy nodded.

Wolflock rolled his eyes and punched his arm. "Idiot."

"Ow! So, what are we doing?"

"Do you think you could cause a distraction while I swing down into the Captain's quarters and go through his logs?"

"I can give it a go. Won't he suspect we're working together though?"

"Very possibly... we need to enlist someone he wouldn't suspect... Hmm.... Someone he trusts.... someone who doesn't know what they're doing..."

He thought for a while and began pacing; because the deck was so large, he was able to pace from one side to the other, making Mothy follow him to listen to his mumbling.

"That's it!" He clicked his fingers.

Mothy could only chase after him as he ran to the dining hall where Slavidus was scanning over the new roster.

"Slavidus!" Wolflock panted as he approached the older man. "I need your advice."

"Oh? Strange coming from you, Mr Felen, but I'll

bite. What can I do for you?"

"I want to know what Captain Blutro said about your relationship with Miss Voof."

Mothy and Slavidus visibly choked with shock.

"See, Mothy may one day have a sweetheart and I want to know how a dignified and sturdy man like the Captain deals with his best man leaving him for a lover."

Slavidus frowned, "I'm not leaving him, boy. Gosh, you're a nuisance lately..."

"So, you haven't spoken to him yet?"

"I... It's none of your business."

"When are you going to talk to him?"

"Off with you, boy. I've no time for your games. Go and play cards or do something of use."

"So, should I go and ask Miss Voof instead?"

Slavidus kicked his feet down and rose above Wolflock. "Don't you dare!"

Wolflock raised his spindly hands trying to mimic surrender. "Of course, I won't. I wouldn't go and talk to her right now."

Slavidus squinted at him, slammed down his mug and stormed off.

"How on Pelaia-?"

"Easy, Mothy. He loves the captain, and he loves his work. He wants to ask Yifi to stay. But he is noble. He'll ask the captain for permission first. He'll bring him up on deck to clear the air, watch the water and keep them both on neutral ground. He'll be terrified if he has to say everything in the Captain's stateroom. That should give us enough time. Now I need you to act as my lookout. Pretend we're playing hide and go seek. Get the children on board to play, too. That will throw them off."

"Be fast, Lockie. I'll start squawking when the Captain leaves the deck."

"I just hope he hasn't learned to lock his balcony door yet."

Wolflock climbed carefully down the stern side of the ship.

A small balcony lit from the inside backed the Captain's stateroom. The doors leading into his room had large glass panels. Wolflock could see through the glittering translucent mosaics that the room was empty. Captain Blutro had taken the bait.

He jiggled the swirling door handle, but it didn't budge. It rattled and shook, but nothing.

He has learned to lock his doors... Wolflock thought bitterly. *I know how to get around this.* He recalled that the latch on the other side wasn't a real lock, but rather, a little stick and hook. All he had to do was lift it. He withdrew his letter opener, grinning as he slid it between the doors and flicked open the latch. *Smart and sneaky. Myna would be... she wouldn't be proud, but she'd be amused.*

He pushed open the door slowly, re-latching it. He intended on sneaking out through the grate under the centre table as he couldn't climb back up onto the top deck the same way he came in. Wolflock began his search. The room was filled with bookcases, which made it difficult to know where to even start. The books were only on shelves from the hip up. The Captain's room also didn't sport a rug. Wolflock noted water damage in certain areas, particularly by the door.

He gets water in here. *I wonder how...*

Shaking off his unnecessary observations, Wolflock pushed his black hair back and jumped up on Captain Blutro's perfectly made bed. It looked like it was carved from polished stone rather than made from fine linen. Wolflock knew he had to take note of that so he could return it to its original state and not be discovered.

Journals.... journals... nautical books.... logs.... Where are you?

He ran his thin finger along the spines, moving from one area to the next. Nothing.

Wolflock looked for any journals that were before the years Blutro Silk was Captain, but while he may have been on the ship in another role. It made sense that he would be on the ship and work his way up to Captain. Along the Captain's uppermost bookshelf were other journals, made of blue leather, but older and worn from use. He reached up and ran his finger along the spines, viewing the name of the Captains engraved on them.

"Blutro Silk, Blutro Silk, Blutro Silk...." he mumbled. "Ah ha!" Wolflock laughed, pulling out three older texts, all with the name of "Silk" engraved on the spine. One in particular had two names across it with one gashed out. The surname was still Silk, but Blutro had inserted his own name, as if this journal had once belonged to someone else. *His father? Grandfather? No. That was Beleur Silk. This journal is for much too short a time. His brother?*

Knowing his time was limited, Wolflock smoothed the bed and climbed under the centre table, opening the first blue dusty book. It fell open to the bookmarked page detailing the Captain's last entry.

Captain's Log, 23rd day of Eolas Revari, 11th Year of King Rayin's Rule

We are not stopping the ship for the drama that has ensued. One of my crew, Geagle, has been found drunk on duty. I ordered him on half rations and deck duties while we located and burned off the supply. It is days like this that make me want to retire. Luckily, they are few and far between. Hopefully, it won't be like when Crete was Captain. Rest father's soul I will never let that occur again. The alcohol has been rid of. Hopefully that will be the last of it....

The entry hadn't been completed.

Wolflock frowned. Hastily, he checked the first entry. Normal. Nothing exciting. He looked at the second book with the gashes across the front and began to flick through it. The handwriting at the start was jagged, printed and shorthanded, so much so in some places it looked like a secret code. Abruptly at the end of the second third it changed to the elegant scrawl of Captain Blutro. The distinct change was alarming, but upon seeing the entry before and after, Wolflock realised why. This was the previous Captain's journal. Captain Blutro's brother.

The last few entries of the previous Captain were nearly illegible even though they were printed. He could only glean certain words like "port", "sails", "lady", "crew", "sick" and "dead", but none made sense. The very last entry was written in heavy bold letters, ripping through to the next page. It was hard to read as the writer's hand seemed to shake terribly, but Wolflock deciphered it.

I NEED MORE. CAN'T NUMB PAIN. GOING TO DIE WITHOUT. MUTINY.

The next entry was Blutro's, a few pages over to avoid the thick seeping ink stains and tears.

Captain's Log, 1st of Nibit'ling Ickst, 2nd Year of King Rayin's Rule

I have replaced Crete as Captain. Father would have preferred this. Crete may be the eldest and this may be my first official log as Captain, but I hope to do a good job by the crew and father's memory. Aujin is my only comfort at this time. The stress is making me lose my hair. Perhaps I shall start to wear Aujin if it all falls out!

Crete has been going mad for months now. He is obsessed with the drinking alcohol now. He gives it to the men as encouragement, but it just makes them violent. I had to leave one man in the hands of the Corl Guard for molesting a lady on his shore leave. Crete just laughed. This is not like him normally. He used to be fair and strict but now he lies, cheats and steals. I had to compensate every passenger on the last trip because they all had missing items. Crete is being held in the fourteenth passenger room until we dock near Plugh, then I shall leave him in the Guard's hands. It breaks my heart to do so as I love my brother dearly, but this can go on no longer. Even as I write this, I have a blackened ey...

The last word trailed off with a splot of ink, only to be followed by the next paragraph.

Crete is dead.
The man guarding him fell asleep... He had a secret stash of booze hidden in the ship and a new boy, Grogen, raised the alarm. I stayed with him after he finished swinging his fists and passed out. Crete died very suddenly. He cried to me about how much of a failure he was as he vomited into a bucket. Then he passed out again. I couldn't bear to see him like this, so I left to make sure the men he attacked were alright. I returned to find his face was blue, and he was dead. The doctor, Leadinson of Delenstore, said he had died choking on his own vomit. I may not write a log tomorrow due to grief. We shall have to see how these things go...

He should have felt vindicated. He should have felt victorious. Wolflock felt like someone had kicked him in the chest. He understood now. He couldn't pity Captain Blutro as he held a significant level of respect for him. But he felt a deep and uncomfortable sorrow for his captain's loss. Gently closing the journal as if it were a coffin. He understood why the Captain acted so unlike himself whenever alcohol was in the room. He would have acted not too differently were he in the Captain's shoes.

Curious about what the Captain meant by "Secret stash", he flicked through the pages until he came to a poorly sketched image of the ship from the bird's-eye view of each deck. Wolflock noted that the walls were coloured differently in certain areas. Some were marked with a circle and others with an X.

It looked like the Captain's brother had been trying to remember his own code and find out where the crew had hidden his stash. Wolflock shook his head. The poor man. The poor Captain. Remembering quickly that he wasn't to feel anything for anyone, he shook off the feelings and slid out from under the table to replace the other two books.

He heard a 'caw-caw' noise, but he was too in thought to fully process it.

That sounds like seagulls... We aren't near the sea... was all he thought. He kept the journal belonging to Crete so he could sketch the diagrams and produce a better map of the ship's secrets. As he reached to put them back, he heard someone jostling a key in the lock.

He dived back under the table, just in time for the door to let in the warm breeze from the cabin deck.

Captain Blutro's shiny boots trod around the room. He scratched at some paper, shuffled some books around on his desk, and generally seemed to go about his captain's duties. It wasn't until he came up to the desk and began pulling out the chair that Wolflock thought he was going to be caught. But just before the captain sat down, someone knocked at his door. Wolflock didn't pay any attention to who it was. He just opened the grate under the table and slid inside. Slowly he wiggled as quietly as he could until he emerged, covered in dust and cobwebs, in the crew's quarters.

He was still in danger though. He knew that if anyone saw him in a non-passenger area, the Captain's full wrath would be laid upon him. He peeked through the grate under the stairs, seeing a few figures moving in the dim light. The crew quarters were used for storage as well as crew possessions and sleeping. But everyone seemed at the other end of the hallway. And by everyone, Wolflock could see two people. One wearing a hood which wasn't uncommon in the chilly autumn air, and the other nearly crying as he looked down on the hooded figure. He couldn't hear what they were saying, but the crewman who Wolflock could just make out to be Geagle, pressed something very silver shiny into the other's hands.

Haatji.

He couldn't see her clearly, but it had to be Haatji. He couldn't hear any footsteps above him. Wolflock waited a moment longer before he took his chances. He dashed out of the little tunnel and ran up the stairs. He didn't let go of his breath until he was in his room and the journal he'd taken was under his pillow. He grinned broadly in triumph. He'd get to the bottom of this and no one would stop him.

After a few moments his breathing slowed. He got up, glanced up and down the hall, shut his door, and threw himself back onto the bed. He began skimming through the drawings of the journal, committing them to memory. The colour code and symbols had to mean something. Perhaps Mothy would help him search the ship for them. Black crosses, blue circles, red squares. What could they mean?

He tucked the book away again and searched for Mothy. He was laughing with Nü on the deck.

"So, you heard the birds?" his friend grinned.

"I thought we were a bit far away from the ocean for seagulls."

"Seagulls?!" Mothy gasped in mock horror. "I was a nightingale!"

"I have something you might be able to help me with."

Wolflock let Nü look as well, as she didn't want to be without company. He wasn't averse to the extra eyes as he encouraged them to help him look at what each symbol meant. He took them both back to his room so they could study in private.

"Oh, I know this!" Mothy exclaimed, pointing to the blue circles. "See these spots? I use these exact spots when I want to sneak up on somebody. They're out of sight, but you can see from them. If I had a little mirror, it would be easy as pie."

"Curious..." Wolflock pinched his chin as Nü stretched her thumb and pinkie to check distances between points. "There is a big red square just inside the captain's stateroom. I wonder..."

"Look! There's another where you said Grogen's hiding spot was. Do you think that the red ones are for crew hiding places?"

Wolflock nodded. The black crosses were the newest markings, covering the red boxes and some blue circles. "He was looking for them... The previous captain wanted to find where his drinking alcohol was being stored and he suspected his crew. The black markings are the places he ruled out. But there aren't nearly enough red squares to show that each crew member had a spot... do they share them?" he mumbled to himself.

"It looks like a game of mah-jong." Nü pointed her clean finger at the page. "See? You have to match the pairs to remove the tile. So, the deeper the ship goes, the closer the pieces get."

"I think you mean further," Mothy nodded.

"Closer, further. You know what I mean."

Wolflock looked at the book. If he were to draw a cross through the entire ship from bow to stern, port side to starboard, he saw that Nü was right. The mirrored layout for the hiding spots formed quadrants, but not in the adjacent ones. There were several locations missing though, but they matched perfectly with the existing ones.

"Perfect. So now we know where all the hiding spots are. Now we just need to know which ones belong to which crew members."

Mothy shifted from foot to foot. "Umm... Lockie... aren't you in enough trouble? Why not just take this information to the Captain and have him search the spots?"

"What?! Mothy are you daft? No. He'll punish me for taking this book. And on top of that, the hiding spots around the ship are to provide the crew members with a sense of agency. Controllable privacy. You wouldn't want them to get upset thinking they have no privacy at all? You've seen their quarters. There's very little privacy to begin with!"

Mothy bit his lip, but he still looked uncomfortable with the notion.

"What if we don't go poking around their hiding holes? What if we just wait for them to go near them or see which crew members approach us? Normally when someone doesn't want you to find something in a room, they'll stand between you and it. Does that sound better? I think that sounds better. Nü? What do you think?"

"Only if we play cards or something. I am bored easily lately. I think we have all been on the ship for a little too long." She sighed, stretching as she stood up.

Over the day, the three of them positioned themselves close to each of the hiding spots. Wolflock couldn't help himself. He had to find them precisely. They were quite ingenious. The elegant scrollwork often hid the seams of the little compartments around the ship. Two were in the taffrail with a little locking mechanism under the railing. One was tucked just under the front mast, while its partner was behind the dining hall. Each crew member except for the ones not on duty, gave their places away just as Wolflock had predicted. They were shooed, chatted to and even smoked on. Hognut came right up to them and blew billows of smoke around them to clear them off.

By the evening they had discovered that none of the top deck locations belonged to Geagle.

"How are you going to find out which one is his if he can't get downstairs?" Mothy asked as they made their way back to Wolflock's room after dinner.

Wolflock glowered. "Oh he'll come. I've already seen him break that rule. We're going to need a distraction."

Wolflock began pacing back and forth along his room. It took him a moment to realise that Mothy and Nü were smirking at one another, waiting for him to notice.

He crossed his arms, looking pointedly at them as he tapped his foot. "Well? Spit it out. We don't have all afternoon."

"Need a distraction, he says," Mothy drawled as he rolled his eyes.

"Going somewhere he should not again," Nü copied his tone and eye rolling.

"Ahem! If you're not going to tell me I'm going to..." he trailed off, his indignation melting away as he realised what they had in mind. "You still have some of the smoke flowers, don't you?"

"He always spoils the surprise!" Mothy pouted,

playfully punching the bed.

Wolflock shook his head a little as if he didn't realise Mothy was joking. "It's a gift. Now! We can't do the same thing as before. That will definitely alert the captain to our plan. No. We will need a disguise... Mothy! How tall are you?"

He already knew, but he wanted Mothy to stand up so he could size him up. "Hmm... yes." he walked around his friend, who posed in different comical stances. Nü tittered with each one.

At least they've made up, Wolflock thought.

"How do you feel about dying your hair black?"

"What?!"

"I have some ink here. It should wash out in a few days. If we trade clothes... yes. Yes, I think this just might work! Now, we're going to need to host an impromptu masquerade ball."

Mothy looked at Nü with a bewildered stare.

"What if Mothy just wears your clothes, puts on a hat and climbs to the crow's nest? I'm sure he can mimic your voice well enough to make people think you are both up there," Nü offered.

"Yeah! That sounds better. Not sure we have time for a ball anyway... or the means to make masks."

Wolflock considered it for a moment and

conceded. "It will be dark too. Very well. Let's change clothes, Mothy. That way we'll be better disguised."

Nü stepped out of the room while the boys stripped to their underwear. Mothy had a bit of trouble doing up Wolflock's shirt, vest and trousers. The way his hands moved, Wolflock suspected that he spent more time dressing others than himself. On the other hand, Wolflock felt quite naked without his fitted clothing. Mothy's baggy trousers felt like they'd catch on everything and his shirt kept sliding down over his shoulders.

"Wolflock... this fabric is beautiful. How do you still feel brave enough to climb rigging and do chores in this?"

Wolflock shrugged as his friend stroked the silver swirls on his vest and pinched at the high thread hemp.

"I'd rather the adventure than the luxury. I'm not going to miss out on one in a lifetime opportunity because my clothes might tear. Clothes can be mended or remade. Moments, my dear Mothy, cannot."

He mixed a bottle of ink with water and Nü came back in to help rinse Mothy's soft blonde hair with the black dye until it held.

"I liked your blonde," Nü sighed as she washed her hands with an ointment that took the ink right out. "Everyone back home has dark hair. Black, brown, blue, green. All very dark. Your hair was like the sun."

Mothy wiped his face to hide his beetroot red blush. Wolflock scratched at the itchy hemp shirt.

"Remind me to get you better clothes. This vest is clearly made for someone shorter and wider than you are, and these trousers could fit so much better around your thighs. It would stop them from falling down so easily. How do you do anything in this?"

"Well, I always say that it's the man that makes the clothes." Mothy laughed and stood up primly, holding out his elbow for Nü to take.

"My lady."

Nü rolled her eyes with a smile.

"You've got to admit, he wears my clothes well." The boys joked simultaneously.

"Neither of you would wear my father's clothes well," she added.

"I will take that bet," Mothy winked.

Wolflock cut through the flirting by handing Mothy his satchel, now filled with smoke flower flares and a bowl with some wheat stalks the cook had taken seeds off. The fresh wheat from the Krieger Zwerg dock had made for some of the lightest, fluffiest bread Wolflock had tasted, but the stalks, he had already noticed, were suitable for Mothy's hair disguise and a wig for himself.

"Why does being you make me so itchy!" he

groaned, scratching his head and waist like a monkey.

"Me and Mothy here will go and set up the distraction, aye?"

"It's Mothy and I," Wolflock corrected. "Just don't let anyone see you up close. You're tanner than me and we have distinctly different faces."

"Most certainly, my good man," Mothy sniffed, raising his nose in the air as he turned on his well-polished heel and exited the room, Nü following smoothly behind him.

It took a few minutes, but Wolflock soon heard the stamping of feet and cheers from the crowd upstairs. As the evening swept over them like a giant river ray, Wolflock could make out the glittering blue lights from their specialised flares.

Confident that everyone was distracted, Wolflock moved into the hallway. No one. Good. He slipped down the stairs, dodging the last one because it creaked. Only two sleeping crew members. Snoring softly, but still snoring as they swung with the sway of the ship. He tiptoed passed them, keeping to the side so he could duck away if anyone entered behind him.

Finally, he made it to the hull stairs. He'd finally have a chance to have a good look through Haatji's cargo and see where the alcohol was hidden.

He counted the places leading up to Haatji's sectioned off area. Wolflock cocked his head to the side.

The dust was thick on her belongings. No one had moved anything to or from here in a long time. There were only two cases stacked on one another. Wolflock stepped over the rope and clicked one suitcase open. He knew it was from his country because of the leather-bound style. Why did a woman from Uluken have suitcases from Grothener? Why did such a wealthy woman have so little on the ship? Her trunks had letters he couldn't read, journals, a painting of a Shiriling man on a canvas rolled up, and a bag of coins. No brown bottles. No letters about trading in alcohol. Nothing that would suggest that Haatji was a wealthy alcohol smuggler.

Wolflock sat back. Had he been wrong this entire time? He stood up and paced, looking at the floor. As he walked around the central ship storage area, he noticed scratch marks. They were deep and fresh, only illuminated by the light from the fairy dust lantern hanging by the stairs.

Something heavy with metal at its base had been dragged across the floor. This was odd for two reasons. One, the ship's crew loved the ship and would never drag someone across the floor. These scratches were possibly the work of a crew member who couldn't lift something heavy. But that wasn't any of them. Each crew member was perfectly capable of lifting a fully loaded barrel, if not two, with ease. Their minds may not have been as acute as Wolflock's, but he had no questions about their physical strength. So, someone who wasn't a crew member had been moving things. Someone who couldn't lift a heavy item. The second odd thing about the scratches was that they weren't leading to the stairs. They seemed to be going from and to random places.

As Wolflock looked around the room, he saw that several containers had been moved from different places. Things had changed. But not in the way he expected. Kneeling down, he drew out the rosewood handled magnifying glass and one of the lanterns from the wall. The scratches lead from the centre. The oldest ones did anyway. They were pulled out to different passenger storage areas. Then fresher scratches put the heavy items back at the crew's storage. Finally, they diminished in frequency and there were only two lots of new scratches. Two lines leading simply to the front of the crew storage and the other leading to Stra's storage area.

Wolflock pinched his chin. Nothing was leading to Stra being the culprit. He hadn't even been in his web. Shaking his head, Wolflock opened the barrel. Low and behold, bottles of alcohol sitting amongst water bobbed before him. He looked around the room again, thinking, rolling one of the wet bottles in his hand.

"If someone has been repeatedly moving the barrels, that would explain why not all of them were found in the Captain's sweep. These two are quite tucked away." He cracked open the lid to check the contents. One was full, but one had a quarter of the bottles missing. Had more been circulated? No. Not yet. They're being stored somewhere. But where?"

As he thought to himself, he recalled the diagrams of hiding spots. Mothy wasn't here to chastise him for digging through the crew's possessions, so he went to work without a second thought. One was under the hull stairs; as he suspected, it was Grogen's, so by Nü's mah-jong rules he knew the other was on the opposite beam.

He quickly found the extra seam of wood, not quite as well hidden as the others on the top deck but obscured enough for anyone not looking for it. It was a rather large area, carving out a significant portion of what looked like a decorative rib of the ship. Wolflock pressed the wood in and it popped out, swinging open easily. A smirked crossed his lips as the brown bottles glittered in front of him.

Eighty in the first barrel and sixty in the second by Stra's storage. Now my final twenty. Perfect.

"Got you." He collected them up. As he drew them

out, he saw an open box with a fabric insert in the shape of a flask. The image of the silvery item Geagle passed to Haatji earlier flashed through his mind. He knew this had to be Geagle's hiding place. It was somewhere he had seen the crewman try to get to before when he helped carry one of Yifi's crates into the hull. Knowing he didn't have much time; he shook the thought from his head for now and took the bottles back to Mothy's hiding spot in the crate at the back of the hull. Wolflock collected up all the bottles in Mothy's baggy shirt and stashed them away. He then did the same with the barrel in Stra's area.

It left him thirsty to work in the dry, dusty air. The bottles became quite heavy after a few trips. After his first trip with twenty bottles, he realised that they were not only very heavy, but awkward and slippery. He reduced the size of his trips, carrying less with each trip. Eventually, just one was left in the barrel.

"Why do you cause such a fuss?" Wolflock asked the bottle casually, curiosity asking him to keep just this one. He heard steps above his head and jumped, nearly dropping the bottle.

He didn't have time to hide the lantern or the bottle. If it was the Captain he'd be in huge trouble. What if the Captain saw that he'd taken the journal? This looked bad. He wouldn't listen to him if he tried to explain himself.

Wolflock felt his throat clench, and he knew all he could do was duck behind the boxes in Stra's storage and pray to the shadows that he would remain concealed.

The light footsteps couldn't be a crew member. Would it be worse if they caught him with a bottle of this stuff on him? Of course, it would! He'd look like the smuggler.

Feeling his heart beat hard against his ribs, Wolflock uncorked the bottle and thought to pour it out on the floor, but then realised that it would smell. He had no choice. He put the rough edge to his lips and gulped. The cold liquid burned his throat, and he stifled a cough, feeling his eyes pour with tears. The footsteps came down further. He gulped again, this time managing to not splutter at all. It was dreadful stuff. His father had let him have a sip of wine before, but at least that had a flavour. This tasted like... Well like hot ice mixed with cleaning liquids.

He continued to drink as quietly as he could while the figure moved from the front of the hull to the centre. He heard wood being pried apart, lids opening and closing, and frustrated sighs. He felt sick. His entire stomach burned, and he thought he was going to throw up. Only a quarter of the bottle remained, but he couldn't do it. It felt like poison. Why would anyone drink this?

He resigned. He had to get rid of the fluid. Maybe

putting just this little bit back in the barrel wouldn't be so bad.

His thoughts started to slow.

Yes. That would work. He just had to do it carefully.

He got up onto his knees behind the barrel. Did the ship sway this much all the time? He wished the Captain would stop spinning it so fast. He glanced over the top of the barrel to see the figure climbing tentatively up onto some crates to check a barrel stacked on top. Old orange curl toed shoes.

Those couldn't be the only ones Haatji wore, surely? She was wealthy, was she not?

He hooked his thumb into the barrel lid and opened it as carefully as he could. He didn't think it made a noise, but the figure began looking around. He held still as their amber eyes glazed over his dark hiding spot. They fixed on the fairy dust lantern he'd laid just across the walkway. As they jumped down, he seized his opportunity, shoving the bottle back into the barrel and squishing his palm down on it to seal it shut. Then he withdrew his arm and pressed his back to the curved wood, holding his breath.

The footsteps of the hooded figure came closer. She tapped her fingers on the wood nervously. It wasn't a rhythmic tapping, but just a random patter. She came closer. Wolflock's head was whooshing, his stomach churned, and the ship felt like it was doing somersaults. Jumping up and shocking her before he ran upstairs sounded like a great idea right now. He didn't know why, but it sounded like something plausible.

He heard her bracelet chink on the metal of the barrel behind him. He swore she could see the top of his head.

Any moment now his legs would work. He'd jump up, scare her and then make a dash for it.

He drew in his breath. The pressure in his chest pushed down the sick feeling.

"What are you doing down here?" Geagle ran down the stairs, galumphing as he moved. "I told ya not ta come down here. I gave ya that present."

"I ran out," the woman whispered. Wolflock couldn't hear a slur.

"That's fine, but we agreed to ration it. I don't want the Captain to know. I don't want you to get in trouble."

"But I ran out!" she hissed more urgently.

"Then bring me the flask and I'll get it."

"But how can you get it if you can't come down here for me? The Captain forbid you from coming under the deck. Who will keep me warm at night?"

Wolflock couldn't help it. He had to see. He had to try to glimpse what was going on. He turned around, peeking between the convex curve of the barrel and box. The hooded figure was wearing the same brown cloak and he could see the glittering gold hathphool bracelet as she stroked Geagle's broad chest.

"I'll just sneak down. It ain't hard to do. I do it for you, my rose. I'd do anything for you."

"Then just give me the hiding spot. Tell me where you keep moving it all too. Or better yet! Let's move it into my room so no one else can find it?"

"I... Well..." Geagle looked around the room and frowned. "Oi. You've moved 'em again! I told you not ta do that. You keep trying to sneak it and I have to move 'em to other spots."

"Well, you moved them away and I had to find them again! Stop moving them and just let me have it."

"No, my sweetheart. Please don't make me do this. C'mon, you know it upsets the Captain."

"Everyone else likes it! He's just got a stick up his-"

"Don't talk about him poorly. He's a good man. He's a good Captain."

"A good Captain would let his passengers and crew have a bit of fun!"

Geagle looked away, biting his lip.

"I... We have to do it with the flask. It's the only way to keep you going until we get to the next port. Listen to me, Honey Muffin. Don't cry. Oh, please don't cry! Look, I'll refill it again today, but I can't do it again before dinner. Aye?"

The woman had wailed, but Wolflock saw no tears in the light when she drew her hands away. Geagle moved to his hiding spot and dislodged the door. Wolflock smiled for a moment, validated that he got the spot right, but his stomach writhed, and he had to sit back down. The spinning ship made him feel even worse, so he closed his eyes. He felt so heavy. Like he was soaked with water.

"Huh? Hey! I told you not to go through this. I trusted you!" Geagle sounded quite upset.

"I didn't go through there!" the woman's voice snapped back. "How could you accuse me of something like that?"

"I stored a bunch of bottles in here and now they're gone! You're the only person who knows about this spot. I showed you because I love you. I can't fill up your flask now."

The woman went quiet.

"He knows..." she whispered, but only Wolflock could hear her.

"I'm going to take you back upstairs and make you a cup of tea. I've got ta get back ta swabbin', but I'll make sure you're all fine first."

Wolflock heard a slap, although all the noises seemed to be drifting further and further away.

"Don't touch me. I'm... I'm going to bed."

"I... aye. I gots ta take ya outta here though."

Wolflock looked up under the stairs and saw them both disappear. Was Haatji onto him? Was he the one that knew? Perhaps he'd go through her things again just to make sure he missed nothing. Something about the arch of this barrel was quite comfortable, though. His heavy closed eyes and the sway of the ship rocked him gently. Was this why people drank alcohol? He was certainly feeling sleepy.

To make sure the ground was still there, he patted the planks beneath him, then the barrel, then the crate to his side. They weren't sliding around; of that he was sure. As he patted the crate, he found a little hole where one of the tree knots had been pushed out. A rat had chewed it. There was a bag of herbs inside. Their spindly, piney needles were leaking out.

Stra better get that fixed.... He thought slowly, pinching at the herb. The next thing he remembered was someone coming down the stairs, but he wasn't sure if it was a dream.

CHAPTER 10

A Drunker Man's Words

Wolflock crawled back to consciousness, his head throbbing. He looked around the dark hull, realising he didn't remember sitting here. He was sitting amongst Parihaan's things. He put his hand back to try to stand up, only to realise he had a shred of paper grasped in it.

Where did this come from?

He flattened it out on the floor in front of him. The ink was rough, scratchy, and the paper looked like it had been torn from a notebook. There were also strange smudges that ran like a crooked ladder up the ripped page.

It was written in the common Puinteylien.

P.

When you get to Krieger Zwerg, make sure the goods get on board. Someone will meet you in Creast for pick up. The boss will be furious if you drink it all again like last time.

Don't mess up.
A.

Wolflock squinted at the note. He was sure he'd been unconscious. How had he continued to search while he was blacked out? How long had he been blacked out for? At least the ship had stopped spinning. It was still rocking too much and his thoughts were foggy, but, as he wobbled to his feet, he saw a blurry image in his mind of his mental web. The paper in his hand stitched a thread he didn't know he had to the centre.

He took tentative steps towards the upper decks. With each step he saw things clearer. Slavidus wasn't smuggling alcohol, he was just trying to reconcile his feelings between loyalty to the captain and the ship and his love for Yifi. At the very most, he had smuggled jewellery. Not a crime.

Yifi had been given a box of goods from all kinds of

suitors from Corl. Because she had feelings for Slavidus, she didn't want to upset him, so she hid them, slowly giving them away as gifts to the passengers.

Nan Ji had overspent and overestimated not only his herbs, but how interested people in the central lands of Puinteyle would be in his remedies. He was acting out due to fear and shame, but even through that he was too honourable to run black market operations.

Froderyk had nearly the opposite problem. He was about to collect a lot of money from the insurance placed on his businesses back in Corl, but his employees would suffer. They needed his innovativeness, but he couldn't return. Again, an honourable man who wouldn't deal in black market wares. Proper introductions solved both issues.

Then there was Geagle, the accomplice in all this. The poor lovesick fool had been distracted by a lady, allowing the unsigned for cargo on board. Then, after the contents had been discovered to be drinking alcohol, Geagle's lady friend distributed it amongst some of the passengers in celebration for Mabon. The lady had been prone to succumbing to the temptation of drinking alcohol before, though, according to the note Wolflock had in his hand. Apparently, Geagle had given her a flask to try to measure her intake, but she'd taken it upon herself to hide her own stash so she could continue drinking. Someone had discovered it, though.

He had to hold on to the railing with both hands as he stumbled up the stairs. No one was in the crew quarters. No one he could see, anyway. Muffled noises seeped through the board from upstairs. Was someone arguing?

Wolflock continued to zigzag until he had another railing to steady himself with. He took two creaky steps up before he stopped.

"Captain, there was something I wanted to talk to you about. It's important."

"Listen, Slavidus, if it's the holiday you asked for again like earlier, I said yes, but we have to wait until we finish our trip back to Shellinden."

"No, sir. It's not that."

Wolflock felt as if he was being washed over with a hazy deja vu. It appeared that Slavidus hadn't mustered the nerve to tell the Captain about him and Yifi earlier and instead passed it off as if he needed a break.

"It looks serious, man. What is it? You know I'll assist any way I can."

Wolflock heard Slavidus swallow.

"I... I believe I am in love, sir."

Silence.

Then- "I see."

"I know it's against the ship's policy, but I genuinely love this woman and... Well... I didn't come for your permission. I came for your advice."

"Go on."

"As you're aware, Miss Yifi was cursed by her mother to be exceptionally beautiful. I... I have in my possession a necklace that would nullify that charm. I want to know from you whether or not you recommend giving it to her."

Wolflock could nearly hear Captain Blutro nodding slowly as he thought.

"Slavidus. You are the best First Mate I've ever had, and I couldn't do without you. I've had a trying time these past few days, but this does not bring me the sadness or anger I can see you expected it to bring. My advice? Do what's right for your beloved. You're a good man. If you were on another ship giving the advice, you'd say the same thing."

"I'm afraid she'll take it and leave."

"And?"

"And I'll be heartbroken and made a fool of."

Captain Blutro laughed from his belly. "Oh, my goodness! So what? You have loved, have you not? Is not the joy of love and the memory good enough? You cannot cage a bird and expect it to sing. Listen, if you love her, give her the trinket. You have acted with integrity and honour. That's what you can control. If she leaves, feel warm that you felt the bliss of love for a while. She isn't a possession or a pet. It's hard, but you have to trust that she will do what makes her most happy."

"I don't think that's the advice I was after... but in a way it is. You're an old cod, Silk."

"When you have time tomorrow, give her your gift. It's getting a bit late to think clearly. It's been making you sit crooked since Mabon."

Wolflock heard the raised voices again, but they were clearer. Nan Ji was yelling at someone on deck.

"What in blue blazes?"

"Don't worry, Captain. I'll sort it out." Slavidus moved down the hallway, leaving the Captain standing by the crew quarter's entrance.

Wolflock took another step higher. It didn't creak, but he did misplace his foot, falling forward and cursing as he bruised his shoulder on the stairs. With an exasperated sigh, Captain Blutro stepped back and looked down at the straw-haired boy.

"Mothy?" he snorted.

"Yeths!" Wolflock pointed a finger up, keeping his head down to hide his face. "It isth I! Muffy!"

Captain Blutro rubbed his thumb between his bushy

grey eyebrows. "Wolflock... I have so many questions."

"I am Moothey!" Wolflock protested, struggling to rise. The Captain hoisted him up by the arm and picked off his wig.

"And I'm a milk maid. What are you doing and why are you talking like that?" he sniffed Wolflock's breath. "Explain. Now."

"I went down to the hull to find more cluesth and I've thsolved it! I. Thsolved. It!"

The Captain's face was irritated to say the least.

"Then when I wasth looking for the things taht hold the liquiss the orange-traitor came down. To avoid any suspicionousness, I drank the bottle I was hiding and then I thsolved it!"

Captain Blutro let him go, thumbing his forehead again. "Why did you drink the alcohol and not just pour it out?"

"Ah!" Wolflock leaned on the wall, but waved his hand triumphantly. "Because that's what they wanted me to do! Then they would have caught me! But I'm far too clever for that. Mark my wordsth thsir!"

"I'll ask one more time. Why did you drink it?"

"For thscience!"

The Captain stayed silent, thinking, taking deep, slow breaths.

"I justh wanted to help. Am I in trouble? I didn't mean to get in trouble."

"You're... By all rights you should be in trouble. But you're not. When you're clearer minded, I'll ask you more about it, but for now, what is the solution to the problem?"

Wolflock brightened up. He looked around surreptitiously and gestured for the Captain to lean in closer.

"The smuggler... is the person with the silver flask."

Captain Blutro raised an eyebrow. "Silver flask, eh?"

Wolflock nodded too fast and made his head spin. "I don' feel s'good, thsir."

"Let's get you some water. That will help." The Captain put a strong hand on Wolflock's shoulder and steered the wobbling teenager to the top deck.

"So, I'm not in trouble?"

"No, Mr Felen. I'm sure you've punished yourself enough."

Wolflock couldn't understand what he meant, but he felt relieved, nonetheless. The Captain helped him walk to the top deck stairs before they both heard a wretched shriek. Without a word they both ran up the stairs. Wolflock stumbled, but was only a step behind.

"How dare you!?" shrieked a woman. The voice was so shrill it was hard to tell who it was.

Wolflock saw the backs of most of the crew and company. He pushed passed them until he could see what was going on, finding an ideal position next to Haatji. He looked her up and down. She was in her evening wear. A matching purple satin headscarf and pyjamas under a shimmering scaled dressing gown cascading down to a pair of clean, new looking curl toed black shoes.

Not orange... She hasn't got any pockets. And this isn't the cloak I saw the smuggler wearing.

"Whath's going on?" he asked her as Parihaan unleashed a torrent of Uluken swears. Nü, Parihaan, Geagle and Nan Ji stood in the centre of the squashed circle the rest of the crew and company had formed around them.

"Geagle said Parihaan was sick and asked Nan Ji to treat her. He refused and told Nü to do it under his instruction, but now Parihaan is refusing to be treated by anyone but Nan Ji." Haatji whispered. Her eyes were clear. She spoke well, except for that slur. No. Not a slur. *A lisp.*

Wolflock wanted to kick himself. It wasn't Haatji. It never was.

"Baba," Nü pleaded, "Just-"

"I will never touch this foul creature!" Nan Ji roared. "She has insulted my honour! She has insulted your mother! Do not cry for me to treat her!"

"Baba, it is your duty," Nü squeaked meekly. Wolflock had never seen her so uncomfortable. "You promised to treat all people on the ship-"

"Or have my children treat them! I will not waste herbs on this-this-this derelict!"

Nü broke away from her father and moved to Parihaan, who slapped her hands away. "Please, ma'am. You are not well. I can help. Just let me-"

"Get off me! Filth!"

Wolflock's eyes shot around the circle and he saw Mothy. His eyes looked browner than they ever had, and his fists shook, but he remained behind the confrontation.

"I will not let your slave children touch me! I will only be treated by a professional and you are not one!"

Geagle took her hand, his eyes filling with tears. "You're not well, Pari-rose. Please let them treat you-"

"GET OFF ME!" she shrieked like a banshee, tearing herself away, but she stumbled towards Wolflock, tripping over her own feet and fell flat on her face. As she fell, Wolflock saw the final piece. His mental web, although hazy from the drinking alcohol, was complete. The silver flask glinted in the ship's torchlight from Parihaan's hip pocket. Instinctively he knelt down to help her up, but his eyes couldn't help but take in everything. She looked up at him with yellow irises, her nose was covered with broken blood vessels, breathing a putrid stench that smelled like acid mixed with pine. She was trembling, but it wasn't a nervous tremble, more like a jitter. Like Mothy said, long-term alcohol drinkers got when they didn't have any for a while. As he took her hand to help her up, she pulled her skirt forward, revealing dusty old orange curl toed shoes.

She had been lurking around the barrels on the dock. She had also been sitting next to Geagle at Mabon. She had only become social when alcohol was introduced on board. She hadn't been able to maintain balance during the Mabon games. She looked horrified when the alcohol was burnt off. She certainly wasn't strong enough to move barrels by herself, therefore having no choice but to leave scratching. Then there was the note addressed to "P." that he had found in the hull.

P for Parihaan.

Everything fit perfectly. Even with his mind feeling like treacle, Wolflock could see that.

"You'll help me, won't you, boy?" she whimpered, clawing up his arm. "You will make the medicine man help me, won't you? You'll make me better, right? You're a smart boy, aren't you? You'll help your good friend, won't you? Oh, won't you help a poor, poor-"

SMACK.

Haatji had launched forward, seizing Parihaan by her arm and slapped her with the back of her right hand. The ship fell deathly silent.

"You are embarrassing yourself. Leave this boy alone! You disgust your ancestors' sands with your behaviour!"

Wolflock blinked, confused at how sandy ancestors could be disgusted with anything.

Parihaan staggered to her feet, standing a few inches taller than Haatji, but cowering enough to shrink back down under the sober woman's height. "How could you?" she breathed, holding her red cheek. "We are sisters. We are both from-"

"I have denounced family who have acted better than you," Haatji spat.

"That is not for you to do! You are a woman! Women are the ones who are denounced! You speak like a man!"

Haatji said nothing, but her face looked like stone.

Everyone seemed too shocked by the altercation to move. Not getting a response, Parihaan continued. "If you had just let me do what women are meant to do none of this would have happened! It is a woman's job... it is my job... to serve the drink! Why would you take that away from me?" She turned, shrieking, towards the Captain, but

Wolflock could see her eyes were unfocused. "Everyone was my friend until you stopped me-" Her eyes cast over Captain Blutro standing between Slavidus and Stra. She froze, all colour drained from her face. Her silence gave Wolflock the chance he needed. He stepped forward, taking her arms and held her kindly. Just like Mothy would have done.

"It's alright. I know it wasth you." He grimaced as he heard his own slur. "You did it all. I just want to understand why. Thisth is very fas-cin-ating to me. I've never met an alcomaholic before. Just accept you did a wrong and we can start over, ye?"

Parihaan looked at him as if her were a river bug larva. "What... what have you been drinking? Have you stolen-"

"Enough!" Captain Blutro stepped forward, his booming voice breaking through the turbulent atmosphere. "I have heard enough."

"But Captain!" Wolflock raised his hand in an attempt to be commanding. "Thisth woman is..." he sighed heavily, lowering his voice, "I'm sure you can be so much better. I know you probably weren't the mastermind in all thisth. You can have friends though. If I can have friends, then anyone can have friends! You don't have to smuggle alcomahol to do it. I mean have it. I mean have them. I mean, you're silly and not too bright and not too wealthy and you probably have a terrible past, but-"

As Wolflock spoke, Parihaan's eyes filled with tears. She looked around at the crew and company, shrinking down. All at once she shoved him aside and ran downstairs.

The Captain stood by him and patted his shoulder. "It's alright, lad. That is not your job. Everyone, Parihaan is under cabin arrest until we sort this out. No one is to communicate with her beside First Mate Slavidus, Second Mate Canhop and myself. Grogen, go help Mr Felen sober up. Miss Haatji, please accompany them. He's being conducting science experiments."

"Sthcience!" Wolflock raised his hand in the air as Grogen sombrely escorted him away.

Wolflock was confused, unsatisfied with the response and didn't know why.

CHAPTER 11
A Sober Man's Thoughts

Grogen's method for 'sobering' Wolflock up was to hold him by his ankles and dunk him into the dishwashing barrel. Coughing and spluttering, Wolflock wriggled like a fish from Grogen's grasp.

"'Here," the towering man snorted, handing Wolflock a jug of water. "S'the only thing for it."

"Ugh..."

As he lifted the cup to his lips, he felt another torrent of icy water pour over him. With a piqued stare, he looked up to see Grogen shrug, unable to hide his smile.

"For good measure."

"Thanks."

His head was certainly clearer, and he was grateful to be wearing Mothy's clothes and not his own. He looked around the dining hall, seeing things more sharply.

"Where is Mothy?"

Grogen shrugged again, tossing him a towel. "Dunno. Most people'ave gone ta bed. S'late, me lad. Feels later than it is..."

"People don't normally fight like that on the ship, do they?"

"Nay. Not normal at all. This whole trip has been odd. Norm'ly they get on, make some friends, do whatever they do and then leave. They're norm'lly more relaxed and easier to handle. Haven't seen that kinda act since I was new on the ship during the last Captain's time."

"That's why Captain Blutro banned alcohol on the ship, isn't it?"

Grogen leaned on the bench, his burly arms propping him up. "Aye. He blames booze for his brother's death. T'weren't that though. The old Captain just... he had some issues he weren't ready to deal with. That, plus the responsibility of running a ship before he was ready. We all try our best, but some people just cope poorly. S'a waste. S'a terrible waste."

Wolflock rubbed his black hair and wrung out

Mothy's shirt as best he could. "Have you drunk alcohol before?"

Grogen shrugged. "A couple-a times. I tried good stuff, bad stuff, mid-range. Not that much difference 'tween 'em all. Couple of the crew used to use it to relax after a shift. I prefer music, though. Music brings me much more comfort than anything ya eat, drink or smoke could bring."

Wolflock felt his headache, but at least he could think now. He seemed to regain control over his mouth, which he found when he smiled at Grogen's sentiment.

Haatji had remained quiet this entire time standing just outside the kitchen space, looking to the door.

"Why did you get so violent?" Wolflock asked her, too tired to interrogate, leaving his tone more like Mothy's.

Haatji shifted her shoulders, looking away. "I... My previous... I... ahem." she swallowed. "Parihaan's behaviour made me think of the kind of woman I had been encouraged to be back in Uluken. I cannot stand for the subservience expected of women around my birth lands. Powerful, intelligent women think they are getting marriage to a good man only to find out that he wants to break them down into the image he sees as fitting. It is not many men, but they seem to have a far-reaching effect."

Her lispy voice was steady, but Wolflock knew that he heard just a shadow of her true rage behind it.

"Yeh didn' need to hit 'er though. Tha' doesn't help nobody." Grogen chided.

Haatji looked away again, her pastel green eyes sparkling with fury. "Am I being forced to remain here?"

Grogen shrugged, "D'ya feel yeh need ta be kept 'ere to be a civil passenger?"

"No."

"Then you're free ta go."

Haatji sighed and took a few steps away but turned and looked back at them.

"I... I am sorry for my behaviour. It will not happen again."

Grogen smiled, but Wolflock could see a sadness in his face. It was as if the ship would be permanently marred by this evening.

No one spoke as Haatji departed. Wolflock watched after her, but he remained quiet. He felt as if he had messed up. Other passengers mindlessly meandered around the dining hall, waiting for the kettle to boil. The slight clink and clatter of the hulk in the kitchen was the only noise to be heard. Grogen poured the tea and passed Wolflock the first cup.

Yifi, Fuhji and Froderyk came over for their own servings.

"How do you fix this?" Wolflock blurted out, his

mind sharp with agitation from the puzzle before him. "How do you solve this crime?"

"Whadaya mean, lad?" Grogen asked as the others stared.

"Well, Parihaan. It's clear she had a problem, right? But it's not a case to solve or an ignorance to correct. It's... what is it?"

Froderyk cleared his throat, handing Fuhji a cup of the steaming bitter green tea. "It's an ailment of the being, lad. When someone is addicted to a substance, an activity, a place, it's because they get love from it. Or..."

"They get a feeling of love," Yifi continued as if she was reading his mind. "I used to be addicted to drinking a special brew one of my suitors gave me. Every day he'd bring me a new bottle, and it didn't matter how much I drank of it, I didn't change in shape or appearance because of my curse. He lusted after me because of it. He was the only one I knew who could bring it to me, so I equated it with love..."

Fuhji put her hand on Yifi's shoulder, but the beautiful woman didn't seem to upset by the memory.

"If I had known that there were people who would let me be myself, who would love me for me. Who accepted my faults and encouraged me to be my best... Well... I learned that eventually."

Wolflock bit his lip, the tea untouched in his hands.

"I used to be addicted to smoke. That ol' plant tobacco. It smokes smooth when you get the good stuff and makes you feel real relaxed, but after a while you need it to feel normal. I used to work on a cargo ship with a mean boss and a meaner crew. Needed it just to get through the day. One day I said 'nuffs enough, and I threw both out. Took guts and a few good friends to put me up for a few weeks, but I was determined to only work in a place that made me happy," Grogen chimed in, taking a big draught of his green tea when he was done.

Froderyk nodded sadly through the discussion. "I... Well... Since we're sharing. One of the reason's Fuhji's family doesn't like me all that much is because I took a lot of their employees. They worked them hard. Too hard. And then they also supplied them with sugars and relaxing herbs. A lot of them couldn't cope without them. When I offered them a new place that wouldn't offer them those things but halved their work hours without halving their pay, they took it up in a heartbeat. But I have seen too many workers around me kill themselves or go mad with substances."

"I... I never knew it was such an issue." Wolflock spoke softly, feeling as if his gut was dripping out of him like a ghost. "Why isn't it spoken about?"

Grogen clapped his shoulder, spilling some of the tea into his lap. "It's a pride thing sometimes. Borderline arrogance. Some people aren't ready to deal with why they're hurting and covering it up with their own brand of medicine. Other people don't know it's a problem. That's how they was raised. And then some people see no way out."

"How do you fix it though?"

"Well, first thing, you gotta love the person unconditionally, but within your boundaries. Not everyone can do that, lad. It takes a strong heart, mind and stomach, as well as some steel framed boundaries."

"It also takes very clear, repeated communication that has to be delivered in a firm but loving way." Yifi interjected.

Wolflock scrunched up his face. "It... How could one person solve this though? It sounds impossible! Adults shouldn't need a nanny..."

The four of them looked between each other, smiling sadly.

"It doesn't take one person, Wolflock. It takes a village. A community. That's why the Royal Court sends out and trains mind and heart doctors. They help teach the different provinces about how to communicate nicely. Some people are just really good at it and they can help teach others. People gotta be open to it though. They have to not think they're always right. No 'my way is the only way' thoughts or nothing." Grogen nodded as if he was talking to a class, himself.

"So... you have to send them to a doctor?"

"No. They have to go to the doctor. They have to make the choice. The only thing you can do is give 'em a space. Somewhere safe where they can be their true selves and not feel like they're gonna be attacked or judged or nothing."

The weight of what Grogen was saying sank heavily onto Wolflock's shoulders. How could he do something when he did not understand what that even looked like? He had always been judged his entire life.

"I... I don't think I can do that. It sounds so hard."

"Yeh not meant to do it, Wolflock!" Grogen chortled. "Yeh just a kid. It's an adult's job. Yeh just meant to learn how to do it from us."

Wolflock drank his tea. The bitter sensation was pleasant and somewhat soothing to his tongue. It was easier to swallow now. He felt it clean his gut.

"I wish I'd had adults explain this to me as a child. Especially around Mabon..."

Grogen laughed, clapping his shoulder again and refilled his cup.

"Yeah. Been meaning to ask about that. You got so flustered on Mabon. What's the go with that? You missed out on some good jokes after you left."

Wolflock's face flushed. "I... You mean you're more worried about me leaving than what I said?"

Grogen scratched his stubbly chin, "To be honest, I don' even remember what yeh said. Just that yeh left."

"I remember you said your writing equipment," Yifi smiled warmly.

"And something 'bout the cauldron on the ship." Froderyk put his two sentus in. "I have to agree with you on that one. The foods been fantastic on board."

"Why thank yeh," Grogen tipped his fingers from his forehead to Froderyk.

Wolflock suddenly felt a lot less silly. "My family always made me feel bad for what I said at Mabon."

"That's mean!" Fuhji gasped, "I am curious about your reasons though."

"Well," he took in a deep breath, "I'm grateful for my writing implements because they were a gift from the Captain because of the first case I solved." He was careful to not mention the circumstances in which he solved them. "Then I was grateful for the fairy dust lanterns because they aren't flammable. They keep the ship safe. And finally, the cauldron was what Nü used to heal everyone when they were sick last week."

As he finished, he felt his cheeks burn again, but just because everyone was staring at him with such endearment across their faces.

"You are so much sweeter than anyone gives you credit for!" Yifi squealed as her and Fuhji squeezed him into a big hug.

"I... What?"

Confused, but feeling lighter, he smiled. "So... with all that being said, what can we do to solve this problem?"

The four of them looked between themselves.

"Well, I think we should all try to make sure Parihaan feels more welcome. Without the need to serve drinks." Grogen spoke slowly.

"What if I taught her how to make my special Korsaki tea? That way she could serve drinks that the Captain approved of?" Fuhji offered.

"And I'll make sure she has someone to bathe and primp with. Heavens knows I have far too many beauty products." Yifi giggled.

"Perfect. If we each take our time and put in some effort, she'll at least have people to lean on."

"But what can I do?" Wolflock asked, frowning. He didn't want to be useless.

Grogen sighed, looking at him sternly. "You need to

find the rest of the booze and bring it to the Captain. I'll tell him we're going to act as a support for her and help her recover, but we can't have a relapse. You're the cleverest lad I know, so I'm trusting you to find it and not drink anymore, yeh hear?"

"Aye, aye!" Wolflock hopped off the bench and took a few steps towards the door. He stopped after a second, turned and smiled back at them. "Umm... it might be a bit late, but... Merry Mabon, everybody."

Glowing, they smiled and waved him off.

Wolflock felt as light as a feather. He could do something helpful. Was this how Mothy felt all the time? Was this why people did charity work? It felt lovely. He had tried so hard to be rude, cruel and stop the crew and company from getting close to him, but in truth, they were good people. He felt safe. It was as if their judgements weren't going to burn his heart.

He practically skipped down the stairs and leaped to the side to stop from crashing into Haatji.

"Whoops! Sorry!" he jumped back. He expected her to eye him suspiciously, but she seemed dazed. "Haatji..." He stopped, collecting his thoughts. "I... Thank you for defending me earlier. Are you well?"

"Huh? Oh. You're welcome, Mr Felen. Thank you. I'm quite fine. I believe I'm just... shaken by this evening's events."

"Oh. Well, please rest well. I would love to chat more about Uluken later. I'm intrigued by that land. I know very little of it, which is odd as it's my country's neighbour."

She nodded slowly, backing into her room. She gave her head a little shake as if her mind caught up with the conversation. "Oh! Oh, yes. Yes, that sounds lovely. Merry part."

"Merry part."

He passed the Nan family's room. The door was just closing, and he could see Nü's dress disappearing into it.

She's up late, he thought.

He could see the Captain and Slavidus talking down the end of the hall, but he thought it best to not disturb them. He tapped on Mothy's door, but there was no answer.

Huh... I wonder where he is...

He moved to Parihaan's door where Goden was sleeping on a stool. Knocking, he waited. No answer. With a frown he opened the door. Her plain room was empty.

She might have slipped down into the hull. She won't find the drinking alcohol where I hid it, but I'd best make sure she's alright.

Finally, he moved into the crew's quarters. Surely his

privileges and freedom to move throughout the ship would have been restored. Especially after he took the Captain the last of the drinking alcohol he'd hidden in Mothy's secret crate. Perhaps Mothy was in there too.

With a new pep in his step he walked through the crew's quarters and came to the hull's staircase. It was brighter than usual. He hopped down the steps and came to the landing between flights. He stopped. Something was wrong.

He could see a shattered fair dust lantern illuminating the space at the bottom of the stairs. It was broken over a crumpled pile of clothes. A crumpled, tangled pile of clothes with arms and legs poking out of it.

Dread crackled through him as he saw the face of the person laying in a deathly still heap amongst the shards of glass and bent metal.

Parihaan.

Die Wolfici

I erwarte so werde nicht er fähig zu etwas während an der Schipp. So I übernehmen so merzur nichter zu gehen so einen aktuelle an der Summerabstammung erfordert. Zuerst, Barta ist nicht ehren teer am so. Dine atwaer hat sich smalich der I erzählt therm so werde, und I glaube so werde er eingenet wettem mehr aut ist sein spelter als Flush kannte hatte hatte so. Ther anfanglich tun nicht kannt der zu so sein thermeber und hat genehmen hat schreibet es an spelwirt. So is bittet zu der therm ert aut therm Schwar während überdet trotrau. Seh hatt sweet sern treibenn zu abenteuerart und I wagzusagen ther hat wagzusagen serden einen geschicht urheber.

Brennan is bet gut. I habe zeugtet einige sen der stallendch zu 'Schis' therm apfelen bei I artischich plaatzdur fumf sem. So is ein spass klinne dem. Ther is gepflegt taglich und frage fumf so hauft. Barta hat nur runterhalt therm sem marchene sen sein abenteuer zu außen therm ein gut laune.

I. machber. habe nur sergenbet micht gedanken zu der Seal gesellschaft umgebung. Nach der Duergermeisteren misteiligtich zustimt so stallich fehlerfter über ther ohren. ther erfel teilnehmer sem der

Felen famale zu frag fumf beratung. Ihr hab prakverlesen mich zu untersuch darunter ihr und beraten an dazu dual ratsel. Burgermeisterin Zuegabel zagen I bin der lichtstarkenet schuleri ihr hab haben sin jahrene und anerkene wet ihr anrufe miche 'gelasen begeisterung'.

I wurde frag sich dine sitzen abenteuere sind firfahrenet, aber sinct di habe nicht nur gedicht hummerherz. I soll vermuten di sind gut ob dat di sind kuellich an dine weg hummerherz. I da hafe is iz der ehemalig.

I wurde schreib mehr, aber Ganna hab fragt mich zu fruhstuck. Schreib mich lehr lihtere ze I kannen ausplaudern alle I kannen sein sein.

Dine direste kirster,

Myna L. Felen

P.S. I wirde zugeben seit sind ringenet dumpf wehe di.

P.P.S. Kun di nehmen miche verwerit schal? I kennt di habe nur weet is af und I kannicht danken zu finde is.

P.P.P.S. Denurseache. I funde is. Ganna haben fand is abernigung gehnst ihr geraumt miche zummer.

About the Author

Rhiannon is the walker between worlds. One foot in Earth, the other constantly stepping into Pelaia. As if gazing into a crystal ball, she sees this other world and all that happens within it with the clarity of someone staring through a veil. It is her purpose in life to transcribe these histories, adventures and mysteries for you to enjoy.

This witchy woman was raised by a fairy who taught her that there are all kinds of magic throughout the world. She taught Rhiannon to withhold judgement because you never truly know another's story. She also taught her that everyone, no matter how flawed, has something to give.

The adventures of Rhiannon's youth lead her through trials and dangers that taught her about the darkness within the world, but it also showed her that anything could be overcome. There was always a way. Surrounded by so much apathy and hopelessness, Rhiannon made it her goal in life to show others the light and that if they could dream it they could do it.

The way she was shown this was through stories.

Stories of friendship, love, adventure, discovery, compassion, understanding, and kindness. All of these stories gave her new friends, new lessons, new life.

In the depths of her darkest place during year 11 and 12, when she felt at her loneliest, drugs surrounded her life in terrible ways, the self worth of those she loved and admired crumbled, she was relentlessly bullied and felt friendless in her most trying years, she lived in squalor due to bureaucratic errors, and yet she still had to be "perfect". She had to perfectly excel in school, she had to perfectly remain calm and gentle in the face of abusive men, she had to be a perfect role model for all those around her. That craving for perfection in order to get love nearly killed her several times. In all of this darkness with politicians sacrificing real people and real environments for imaginary money, with teachers displaying no compassion for their students, with men abusing women and children, with communities vilifying those who needed them most, with injustice reigning and all hope seemingly lost... Puinteyle was born.

All of these pains in life were fixed in Puinteyle.

All of them were able to be mended and healed because of a conscientious effort. The people of Puinteyle wanted to be better than their problems. Puinteyle was where people made an effort to love freely and always sought to help each other, animals and the environment. Harmony. True and beautiful harmony. Where the pendulum never swayed too far away from that beautiful harmonious and happy point of balance.

But like in our lives, there is always obstacles to overcome and darkness to understand. Therefore, Puinteyle would always have its own inner turmoils to learn and grow from too. Thus, the stories never truly end.

Rhiannon has always lived and breathed stories, knowing her role in life is to be this guide through a new world for others. Her dream is to support her community with her stories, as well as creating a company where other artists can come together in celebration of Pelaia and all it has to offer.

Get More of the Magic & Mystery...

subscribe.rhiannoneltonauthor.com/more

If you want more clues, more magic and more mystery, let me know by going to the Case of the Bitter Draught subscribe page.

You'll get clues, maps, sketches, behind the scenes stories, lore and much more! You'll also be the first to know when a new story is coming out so you can solve the mystery before your friends.

If you sign up with the magical link below, you'll also get a free downloadable map to follow Wolflock's journey to Mystentine University.

subscribe.rhiannoneltonauthor.com/more

If you enjoyed this book, please leave a positive review online (where you purchased the book or on Goodreads), recommend this book to your friends or family, or purchase another copy to gift to a loved one.

Stay tuned for the next mystery in the series:

THE WOLFLOCK CASES

BOOK 5

A STUDY IN SILVER

www.rhiannoneltonauthor.com

 RhiDElton

 RhiannonEltonAuthor

 RhiDElton

 rhiannoneltonauthor

 Rhiannon D. Elton

 RhiDElton

THE WOLFLOCK CASES

1. The Case of the Captain's Hair - Now Available

2. The Case of Mothy - Now Available

3. The Case of the Curse of Houl - Now Available

4. The Case of the Bitter Draught – Now Available

5. The Study in Silver - December 2020

6. The Case of the Lost Mermaid - March 2021

7. The Case of the Pisces Moon - May 2021

8. The Case of the Haemophageous Equine - July 2021

9. The Case of the Lost Antrum - September 2021

10. The Case of the Mountain's Monster - December 2021